Christmas Shadow

The Shadow Walker - Lycan Hybrid Second Generation Series

Book One

Caryn Moya Block

Published by Caryn M. Block
Copyright © 2018 Caryn M. Block

Cover Design by Caryn Moya Block
Model Photo by Hot Damn Design

ISBN-13: 978-0997782912
Library of Congress Catalog Number: 2018913576
Printed in the United States of America

Table of Contents

Dedication

To all the readers that asked for the stories of my character's children. This one is for you with love and appreciation. I have the best readers/fans in the world!

Christmas Shadow

Aleksei Sokolov, a Shadow Walker-Lycan Hybrid, is trying to protect his best friend, Daven McCloud. He installs an Isanti security system in Daven's Beverly Hills estate and assumes his identity. Stepping into Daven's shoes puts him directly in the path of a killer, but it also puts him in the path of Sheridan Harbrook, who has been contracted to decorate Daven's estate for Christmas.

One whiff of her elusive scent and Aleksei thinks he's found his mate, but where is the Lycan Heartmate Bond? How could he be falling in love with a woman who isn't his mate?

Sheridan Harbrook is struggling to care for her terminally ill mother and keep her business afloat. She has no time for anything else, let alone love. She's seen Daven McCloud at parties before and thought him an immature playboy. Despite his reputation, she agrees to decorate his estate for his company's annual Christmas gala.

When she meets with the man she believes is Daven, she can't help but be surprised at how different he is when he doesn't have a starlet on his arm. Feeling that she's misjudged him, she lets him kiss her goodnight, even though the evening was strictly business.

She likes the man and one kiss tells her she could *more* than like him. But as their relationship progresses, danger surrounds them both. Will involving herself with a client put her in the crosshairs of a murderer and will this Christmas be her last?

Chapter One

"Look out!" someone shouted.

Daven McCloud glanced up from his cell phone to see a portion of the brick garden wall topple toward him. He dove away and landed on top of several bushes. Bricks landed around him some bouncing off his lower legs. He groaned. There would be bruises.

"Sir, are you all right?" one of the gardeners of the Beverly Hills, California estate asked, holding out his hand.

Daven lifted himself up thankful for the man's help.

"I'm not dead," Daven answered with a rueful grin. *But, I think I'm in trouble.*

"I'm so sorry, sir," the gardener continued. "Do you need help into the house?"

"Give me a moment," Daven said, trying to regain his equilibrium. He trembled from the adrenalin rush that saved his life. He walked over to a garden bench and sat. "You can go. I'll be fine."

"I'll get some men to fix the wall right away. I'm not sure how it could have fallen like that." The man shook his head and wrung his hands.

"An accident I'm sure," Daven said.

The man nodded and hurried off. Daven sighed and looked at the phone still clutched in his hand. There was only one person he trusted to call with this kind of news.

Too bad so much time had passed since he'd reached out to his old college buddy. He dialed his friend's private number and then stood and moved closer to the shadows along the north wall, stopping next to the open door of the pool house. What happened next needed to be kept secret.

"Daven, it's been a while brother. How are you?" Aleksei Sokolov asked.

"Alek, I hate to do this but I need your help." Daven felt acid start to crawl up his esophagus. He coughed. *Would Aleksei believe him?*

"You sound worried. What's the matter? Girl trouble? I saw your picture with that blonde actress," Aleksei said, teasing.

"It's a little more serious than that," Daven replied, quietly. "Could you come over? I'm in the pool house, north side of the estate."

"What is this about, Daven?" Aleksei asked, his tone serious now.

"Someone is trying to kill me," Daven said, with a sigh. *Saying it out loud made it all the more real.*

"I'll be there in three minutes. Get ready to Shadow Walk," Aleksei said, and then the phone went quiet.

Shadow walking was the special ability of the Nuni Nagi Tribe. It entailed stepping into a dimension next to earth and traveling from one point to another almost instantaneously, but that was only one of Aleksei's special abilities. Daven's best friend could also shapeshift into a wolf.

"Damn, what am I going to do?" Daven murmured.

The strange accidents that had been plaguing his family were coming closer together. First, his father had been killed in a skiing accident in the Alps two years ago. Then, his mother and her new boyfriend had driven her sports car over a cliff in Monaco last year. Now, he seemed to be having accidents. The last one had been a near miss when the brakes on his car gave out two weeks ago. The mechanic had said it looked like the brake line had been tampered with.

Today the wall fell. True, his parents had let the family estate fall into disrepair but Daven didn't think the wall falling was accidental.

He shook his head and walked into the pool house and placed his keys, wallet, change, and cell phone inside the table drawer. His clothes were 100% cotton so he didn't need to worry about them disintegrating in the Shadow Dimension. He glanced at his watch and then placed it in the drawer as well. Looking around again to make sure no one lurked, he walked back over to the shadows.

Aleksei worked for the family business, Isanti, Incorporated. When they first met in college, Daven thought their friendship would be fun for laughs, because he and Aleksei looked enough alike to be twins. But it turned out Daven had found a true friend in Aleksei. One who had shared himself and his family unconditionally.

He was more than Daven's best friend, they were blood brothers. They performed the ceremony one night their freshman year of college during Spring Break after drinking way too much. They stood or rather leaned over the tribal alter in the medicine circle on the tribal lands in Montana. Aleksei's grandfather, Isanti, had appeared out of the shadows and grabbed the wrists they had cut and tied together. He had asked something of Aleksei in a language Daven didn't recognize. Whatever answer Aleksei had given seemed to satisfy his grandfather. Isanti had then turned his gaze on Daven. Daven felt weighed and measured, and had realized, suddenly, he was completely sober.

"Now you are my brother, as well as my best friend, and a member of the tribe. It has been witnessed and blessed by the Great Spirit." The words Aleksei said that night still rang in his mind.

Daven didn't know at the time what all that entailed but by the end of the week he had been given the tribal history and taught his responsibilities to the tribe and his tribal family. He found a new depth within himself as he realized what a gift Aleksei had given him and how much he didn't want to let him down.

Maybe if he requested Isanti, Inc. to set up a new security system in and around the house and hired them as bodyguards, they could get to the bottom of who was behind these accidents.

Suddenly, one shadow separated from the others and became a man. It was always something of a shock seeing Aleksei after an absence. It was like looking in a mirror.

Aleksei grabbed his arm and tugged. Then the dark and cold hit. It was *always* cold in Shadow. Next thing he knew, Daven stood in Isanti's New Mexico office. The blazing sunshine poured through the windows chasing the cold of Shadow away.

Aleksei grabbed him in a bear hug and then stepped back searching his face. Aleksei's blue eyes were a slightly darker shade of blue than Daven's but that wasn't the only difference. Aleksei's eyes would turn golden at times when he drew on his wolf spirit.

Daven had thought shapeshifters to be something in storybooks but when he had become Aleksei's blood brother he had learned all of his secrets as well.

Before, when Daven and Aleksei tried to play their twin trick, Daven had always wondered why they could never fool Aleksei's parents. They fooled his own parents so many times it had stopped being fun. Afterwards, he realized his scent gave him away to Aleksei's parents.

They had tried the twin trick a couple of times after that, with both of them wearing the same cologne but it didn't work. In a way Daven was glad. Aleksei's family really saw him and who he was because they loved him.

When dating in college, anytime a girl said she loved Daven or Aleksei, they would test her with the twin trick. If she couldn't tell them apart, then they knew she wasn't the right one. So far, they were both single.

"Sit down, Daven, and tell me what's going on." Aleksei led him over to a table with two wingback chairs. "Want some coffee? I can have some sent in, or how about a sandwich? I was about to have lunch."

"Sure, whatever you're having," Daven said, chuckling. "I'm starving, I didn't eat breakfast this morning."

Aleksei and his family were always feeding him, and with New Mexico being an hour later, it was near lunch.

§

Aleksei looked into his best friend's face. He saw the worry around the eyes and the way Daven's mouth was held in a thin line.

He and Daven were both around six-feet-tall and both weighed about 190 pounds. Even now, they could still wear each-others clothes. Their hair was the same color, though Aleksei could see Daven had been getting some sun in California, because his skin was tanned and his blond hair bleached lighter.

Daven's hair was also short and impeccably styled, very GQ, while Aleksei had let his hair go and it curled up around his collar.

"I heard about your mother. I'm sorry I couldn't get away for the memorial service. Did you get the note I sent?" Aleksei asked, as he went over to his desk and placed their lunch order.

"Yes, I got it. The flowers were nice too, though you shouldn't have. Mom always thought you were a nuisance, but that's what she thought about me too, so you're in good company." Daven paused. "I'm sorry about not calling you back, Alek. I've been so busy trying to figure out how my parents could almost bankrupt themselves. I let life get in the way," Daven said, sighing.

"Hey, it's okay. You sound unhappy. You must have your hands full." Alex looked toward the door, sensing someone's approach. "Here's Janet with lunch. Let's eat and you can tell me the rest of it," Aleksei said. His secretary put lunch on the table and then prepared to leave.

"Janet hold all my calls and clear my schedule for the rest of today," Aleksei told her as he sat down.

"Yes, sir," she said, looking back and forth between Daven and Aleksei before leaving.

Aleksei took a bite of his sandwich. "So why do you think someone is trying to kill you?"

He listened carefully and occasionally asked a question to clarify. He hadn't known Daven's parents had left such a mess but he wasn't overly surprised. They were irresponsible parents and it made sense that they were irresponsible in business as well.

Daven, however, had a talent in business that Aleksei suspected was psychic in nature. He could see patterns to predict markets and future profits. His gift carried over into other areas as well. He could sometimes predict a person's future after meeting them and knowing their background. It wasn't farseeing or visions, it was all patterns and what made a person behave a certain way.

If Daven wanted to turn his parent's finances around he could do it. But like a dog with a bone, Daven would not let go of the puzzle of why the business was like it was until he had all the answers. It sounded like someone didn't want him to find his answers. The tampered brake line was a dead giveaway, even the falling wall was suspicious. Aleksei agreed with Daven, someone wanted him out of the way. Now the questions were who and why?

"Where would you like me to start?" Aleksei asked. Daven would see the patterns and give him the best place to begin.

"I want to hire Isanti. First, I want contractors to come out and assess and fix any repairs needed done. I need Isanti to run background checks on the repair crews. I want a state-of-the-art security system put into place with a safe room. I want only Isanti employees to be involved, no outsiders. I'll let the household staff go, but please run checks on them as well, just in case. We'll need to screen the replacements, of course. Once the house is safe, we'll start on the business," Daven said, as he ran his fingers through his hair.

"Is the business worth saving? Have you had any offers to buy you out?" Aleksei asked.

Daven shook his head. "I sometimes wish Dad had never invested his retirement in this company. No one has approached me that would send a red flag, if that's what you mean. As far as the business goes, the company just received several government contracts for weapons components. We hold a patent on a guidance system microchip. If we can fulfill the contract then the business would be back in the black. And with some new management, and me behind the wheel, I think I can turn it around," Daven said.

"What kind of time table do we have?" Aleksei asked.

"The board makes its official announcement of my taking over as CEO at the big Christmas Party, scheduled to be held at the estate on December 20th. That gives us six weeks to get the house ready.

"I hired a party coordinator to do the staging and food. She's very successful in Los Angeles. Her name is Sheridan Harbrook. Her company is called "Enchanted Evenings". I checked her and Enchanted Evenings out myself. I don't believe she has any ties to what is going on. What do you think?" Daven asked.

"If *you've* checked her out, she is probably okay. We'll see if anything comes up during our inquiries. What did you find out?" Aleksei asked.

"Sheridan's an only child, who moved back to LA after college to take care of her Mom. Her father died in a car accident a couple of years ago. She took her inheritance and started this business. She had a couple of noteworthy successes and now seems to be doing well. She is accepted by old money as well as new," Daven said.

Just then the door to Aleksei's office opened and without introduction, Penny Running Bear, a woman with copper hair and long legs, came striding in and over to the table.

"I'm sorry to interrupt your meeting, Aleksei, but I *must* have your signature on these purchase orders today," she said firmly, handing him the papers and a pen.

Penny didn't seem to notice that Daven was in the room but the sudden smell of arousal was not because of Aleksei. She only *pretended* not to notice Daven.

Daven looked like someone hit him over the head. His gaze couldn't seem to take in enough of Penny and his mouth hung open making him look like an idiot. Aleksei smothered a laugh. Penny was the daughter of Joe and

Jessica Running Bear. Her older brother, Joe, the third, helped manage the security department of Isanti.

"Penny, this is my best friend, Daven McCloud," Aleksei said. "Daven, this is Penny Running Bear."

Penny smiled and held out her hand to shake Daven's. "Nice to meet you."

"The pleasure is mine," Daven answered. Penny blushed and Daven released her hand *very* slowly.

"Penny, we're going to be doing some work at Daven's house in Beverly Hills. I know it's asking a lot but do you think you could come out with us? We should have you home before Christmas," Aleksei said.

"That sounds great, I'm tired of Montana snow and New Mexico desert. Promise me some fresh seafood and a shopping trip to Rodeo Drive and I'm all yours," Penny said. Aleksei noticed she looked at Daven when she answered.

"Penny, I need you to prepare a security package, class A, with cameras and safe room controls prepped and shipped to Daven's house ASAP. I'll email you the address. Ship it overnight, I want to begin installing tomorrow depending on what repairs are discovered. Also, pack suitcases for two weeks and express them as well. I'll be back for you tomorrow. We'll be Shadow Walking, so be careful what you wear. Get me our best architect and have him available to join us tomorrow as well as an installation team. Let's say eleven AM. Ask Janet to pack me an overnight bag. If I need anything else, I'll let you know," Aleksei said.

At first, Penny seemed taken aback by Aleksei's rapid fire tasks and assignments, but she quickly processed everything he said and began working the details. One of Penny's gifts was an eidetic memory. She remembered everything she saw as well as heard and would get working on his request right away.

She smiled. "I'll see you tomorrow at eleven, then."

She breezed out of the room. Daven shook himself, almost like waking from a dream. Aleksei smiled. His friend had it bad but Penny wouldn't do anything about it unless she was sure Daven was her perfect mate.

Aleksei's mind returned to the problem at hand and needed to get Daven refocused as well.

"Daven, I need you to fire the household staff before we get back. Can your lawyer get over to your place and let them go? Do you owe any of them severance packages?" Aleksei asked.

"I can call my lawyer right away. Knowing my parents, I doubt they even had to give a reason to let someone go. I'll tell him to give them two-weeks' pay and a nice recommendation."

"Have him call when the house is empty. We'll Shadow Walk back when the coast is clear. I'm coming with you and we're going to play your favorite twin trick. I don't want anyone realizing there are two of us. We'll dress alike and I'll take your place at times."

"Alek, are you sure you want to do that? If someone is trying to kill me, they could also kill you."

"You know it's harder to kill Shadow Walkers, not to mention Lycans. Speaking of which, we need a large dog collar."

"You wear a collar now?" Daven asked, chuckling.

"My sister's idea, she figures someone won't shoot us if they see a collar on us. They'll think we're just a big dog. Come on, I need a haircut to match yours and a tanning session. We'll go into Albuquerque."

§

Aleksei drove them into town and the rest of the afternoon was spent making Aleksei look exactly like Daven.

They also bought a big neon orange dog collar with reflector strips. Daven couldn't wait to see Aleksei's big black wolf with the collar. He realized that this was the first time in ages he had been able to relax. He and Aleksei had fallen back into their old camaraderie. Daven found it very comforting. Calling Aleksei had been the right thing to do.

Now if he could get Penny Running Bear out of his mind. He couldn't believe the punch of lust that had hit him when she walked in the room. Daven had wanted to fall into those emerald eyes of hers while he buried his hands into her copper tresses and kissed the breath right out of her.

His body responded just thinking about her. He hadn't had a reaction to a woman like this since college. *Wasn't he too old for this kind of thing?* Even the starlets he had been taking out recently paled in comparison.

When they were done remaking Aleksei they drove back to Isanti, Inc.

They parked and were walking into the main lobby when Penny came rushing up. *Did that woman ever slow down?*

She had changed her clothes from the pale grey business suit she wore earlier to an emerald green sweater and black pants. She looked softer with her hair down around her shoulders and her attire more relaxed. Daven pictured another man putting his hands on her and a wave of jealousy threatened to overwhelm him. He stood frozen, afraid to move incase he did something stupid, like start yelling like a lunatic.

"Aleksei, the package and suitcases are on their way. I added a security package class C to your order, I think you'll probably need the extra cameras. I also added hidden cameras and an audio package. The installation team will be ready at eleven. Before I leave for the day, is there anything else I can do for you?" she asked.

Daven wanted to grab her and kiss her with such force that he held his hands clenched into fists at his sides to stop himself from touching her.

"That sounds great, Penny. Why the extra equipment?" Aleksei asked, glancing at Daven with a frown.

"Well, once I received your email with the address, I did a web search and then a satellite scan. The estate is huge. I'm not even sure the extra package will be enough.

I also added some motion sensors for the estates remote areas and blindspots," she replied.

Aleksei laughed. "Great job, Penny."

"Thank you." Penny turned toward Daven as if she hadn't noticed him standing there. "Mr. McCloud, your lawyer, Mr. Ames called and said the house in now clear."

§

Aleksei saw the grimace on his friend's face and if he wasn't mistaken, the smell of his friend's arousal, along with the bitter scent of jealousy. Daven's hands were fisted at his sides and Aleksei could detect a slight tremble.

Penny didn't seem to react to Daven's discomfort, probably because she didn't have any Lycan in her background, nor did she wait for an answer. "Well, I really need to run, I have a dinner engagement." She turned and walked away.

Aleksei heard his friend swear under his breath and decided to help him out.

"Give my love to your parents," he called after her, hoping to diffuse some of Daven's distress.

"Okay, see you tomorrow," she called back.

They walked back to Aleksei's office in silence. Daven relaxed after hearing Penny was going out with family. *It would be great if they could get together.* Penny never ignored someone like she had Daven. Looked like they both had it bad. He wondered who would give in first. His lips curved ever slightly upward. Maybe they just needed a little Christmas Magic.

"While you call Ames, I'm going to talk to Raven. I'll be back in a few." Aleksei waited for his friend to reach for the door handle to his office before he moved off down the hall to his uncle's office and knocked.

"Come," Raven called.

Aleksei opened the door and stepped inside. Raven looked up from his desk and grinned. Aleksei couldn't help but smile back. His uncle's black hair had streaks of silver showing but no one would guess he had grown children of his own.

"Hey Alec, I hear you're taking a job in California. Nice tan and haircut."

"News travels fast."

"Only because its family. Tell me what's going on."

Aleksei sat down and gave Raven a brief report, including his suspicions that Daven and Penny might have something brewing.

Raven listened with interest, especially when Aleksei mentioned the attempts on Daven's life.

"I understand why you're going, but be careful. Your mother's wolf would rip my throat out if anything happened to you," he said with affection. "Take one of the new keypad systems for the doors. They can be keyed to your DNA, a double lock so to speak. Watch over Penny. Joe is very protective of his daughter. Isanti is becoming a regular dynasty with everyone related to someone."

Aleksei said his goodbyes and headed back to his office. When he arrived at the door he heard arguing inside. He walked inside to find Penny and Daven almost nose to nose.

"Really, Mr. McCloud, you are being over protective and unreasonable. And it's not even yours!" Penny said.

"It is *not* unreasonable to be concerned for your safety, Miss Running Bear. I cannot allow you to put yourself at risk."

"You cannot *allow* it? Who do you think you are?"

"The man you seem to be driving insane." Daven grabbed Penny and kissed her hard.

Aleksei watched very carefully. Penny seemed to be giving as much as she got. He would have stopped Daven, if Penny had shown the slightest hesitation.

Daven seemed to realize he manhandled a woman and pulled back, holding her at arm's length. "Oh my god, Penny. I'm so sorry. Are you okay? I never should have done that. It was totally inappropriate. Tell me you're okay," Daven begged.

"I'm okay. Better than okay," Penny said, wrapping her arms around Daven's neck and stepping closer. He rubbed her back and murmured to her.

Aleksei smiled in supreme satisfaction. His best friend had found his mate, and if he wasn't mistaken by the way Penny held onto Daven, she wasn't going to ever let go.

Aleksei cleared his throat and walked further into the room.

"Well, this changes a number of things. Penny, is Daven your mate?"

She nodded, rubbing the shoulder holding her tribal tattoo. She smiled.

"Then I would suggest Daven, you stay here with Penny. I'll take your place in Beverly Hills. I have an apartment here you can stay in. Feel free to use my clothes. There is room service available so you won't starve. Penny, I believe you get an automatic paid week of vacation time during mating. I'll clear the leave with Raven," Aleksei said, as he walked up to his desk.

"Alek, I can't let you do this alone," Daven said.

Aleksei noticed that Daven and Penny clutched each other, like they were afraid the other would disappear if they let go.

"Daven we've talked about how Shadow Walkers and Lycans mate differently than regular humans, but I don't know if we've talked about the actual bonding process.

"You're going to *need* to be with Penny. Your every thought will be centered on your woman. You will be prone to possessiveness and jealousy until you finish bonding with her telepathically. There is a mating ceremony in front of the tribe, but that could probably be delayed for now

"I can't take the chance on letting you go home when your mind isn't on the danger," Aleksei said.

"You need to take a security detail with you," Daven said. "*You're* the one in danger. I'll start checking and monitoring the business side of things here. I have remote access into most of the computer systems. Penny can help me. If there is someone trying to get away with something, from a business or hacking angle, we'll find it and call you.

"My phone, keys, wallet, and watch are in the table drawer in the pool house. I put them there right before you arrived. I keep my appointment book inside my phone. The passcode is our birth year and the year we graduated from college. The only meetings that can't be canceled are the ones with Sheridan Harbrook. The board is a done deal. So, they shouldn't be calling you on anything. But, please take someone with you."

"Yes, Aleksei, take someone, please," Penny said. "I'm sorry I messed everything up. But, I'm not sorry I found out Daven is mine," she added emphatically.

"With the house empty, I should be okay tonight. I want to get a feel for the place and planned on going wolf anyway. Tomorrow, when I come back for the team, we'll add a couple of security guards. Penny, send out two of the new keypad entry systems. Before they go out, make sure Daven's and your DNA is entered. When we're sure the house is secure, we'll talk about when you can move back in. Now, what was that argument about?" Aleksei asked.

He wasn't surprised when Penny blushed and lowered her eyes. "I wanted to borrow your car. Mine has a dead battery," Penny said.

"You don't drive a stick shift," Aleksei said.

"That's what Daven got upset about," Penny admitted, a little sheepishly.

"Well, he's right. I would never have let you take my car by yourself. Not until I knew you could handle it," Aleksei said.

"I didn't think it would be that hard," Penny replied.

"Not hard but it does take practice and there is a learning process, so no you cannot drive my car."

"My dinner...." Penny argued.

"If you still want to go then Daven can drive you, or you could see if one of the company cars is available."

"Would you like to join me for dinner?" Penny asked Daven almost shyly. "I'm supposed to meet my family at a little Mexican restaurant in town."

"Penny, now that I've found you, I go where you go," Daven said.

"Not to break up this adorable display but I thought of a question. Has anything changed with the plan? Now, that you have Penny?" Aleksei asked.

"Alek, whoever this is will be getting away with murder if we don't go after him. Penny, it's dangerous, but I want you to work beside me to save my family business. I have a feeling that with you by my side, we can accomplish anything," Daven said, brushing her hair back over her shoulder.

"Now that I have found you, I definitely want to help figure out who is trying to murder you. Let's work on that first and then we'll decide the rest," Penny said.

"All right then. I'll see you at eleven tomorrow. Wow, meeting the parents on the first date. Should be interesting. Have a good dinner," Aleksei said, waving them away and tossing the keys. "Daven, here...." He walked into the Shadow Dimension as Daven caught the keys out of the air.

Chapter Two

Aleksei walked out of Shadow and into the pool house. He retrieved Daven's cell phone and watch, and then put the keys and change into his pocket. He glanced at the appointment calendar and saw that Daven was supposed to meet with Sheridan Harbrook tonight. Luckily, he gained an hour by coming through Shadow. Aleksei figured Daven would probably dress for a business dinner, so he headed inside. He listened a moment, using his Lycan senses. The house seemed very quiet. The house staff must have cleared out as Daven's lawyer reported.

He closed and locked the door behind him. Then he did a quick survey of the building, making sure all the doors and windows were secure. He finished upstairs in the master suite. Daven must have redecorated after his parent's death. Aleksei didn't recognize any of the current furnishings. He found a light weight grey business suit in the walk-in closet and changed. He had just finished when the doorbell rang downstairs. He hurried to the door and looked out the peep hole. A woman stood on the landing. He opened the door casually and looked around carefully. She seemed to be alone.

"Miss Harbrook?" he asked, looking at her for the first time. *I should have looked her up on the internet before coming.*

"Mr. McCloud, may I come in?" she asked.

"Why?" Aleksei asked.

"So, I can see the space, Mr. McCloud. You invited me to come over for dinner and see the space," she said, a look of confusion appearing on her face.

Aleksei grimaced. He already messed things up. "I'm sorry, Miss Harbrook, but I find myself without any

23

household staff. I thought maybe we could go out to dinner," he explained.

"I really need to see the space, Mr. McCloud, and please call me, Sheridan," she said, smiling in encouragement. *She has a lovely smile, very open and warm.* He especially liked her hazel eyes that looked like golden citrines. Her hair fell gently over her shoulders in soft auburn waves. Where Penny's hair was copper, Sheridan's hair was a dark deep red. She wore an off-white silk business jacket and skirt with a silky golden top that matched her eyes. Aleksei came to a decision and opened the door wider.

"Please come in, Sheridan," he said, standing back so she could walk past him. *She smells like wild flowers.* He closed the door and locked it.

"I could come back tomorrow, if this is inconvenient," she offered.

"No, tomorrow I have a work crew coming to do a few jobs around the place. That's why there is no staff," Aleksei explained, hoping that it didn't sound too crazy.

"Remodeling, now? But there's only six weeks until the party. Will the work be finished in time?" she asked, real concern in her tone.

"That's the plan. Now where would you like to start?" he asked.

"Well, just the downstairs is contracted to be decorated. Did you have a preference as to the kind of decorations we should use?"

"Kind of decorations?"

"Is there a theme you would like? Perhaps a Country Christmas, or Victorian Christmas, or maybe a more modern theme?"

"Miss Sheridan, you may do whatever you feel is best. The board of Harper and McCloud Industries will be announcing my appointment as CEO, so perhaps a seasonal celebratory look?"

"Celebratory? Hhmm, yes, I think I have a few ideas. What about the greenery?"

"I abhor plastic, so as long as its live, I don't care."

"How many trees do you want?"

Aleksei looked around. If he lived here, where would he want his Christmas trees? This party was important to Daven and if he was honest, Aleksei liked being here with Sheridan. "Shall we go room to room and then maybe we can get a feel for the best placement," he suggested.

"That sounds perfect, Mr. McCloud."

"Please call me...Daven," Aleksei said. He had almost said Alek. *What's wrong with you?* For some reason, he didn't like lying to this woman, and he certainly didn't want her to call him, Daven. The subtle perfume she wore caused him to have some strange desires. Maybe it was because his best friend had found his mate today. Whatever the reason, he found Miss Sheridan Harbrook delicious.

They toured the whole bottom floor discussing where to set garlands of greenery and trees. She made notes in her tablet and took photos for reference as they went from room to room. They decided a large tree in the formal living room and two small trees, one in the den and one in the library. Outside, lighted topiaries would line the drive and be placed strategically around the pool.

When they arrived back at the front door, Aleksei realized he didn't want her to leave.

"I'll come back with samples of ribbon and ornaments for your final approval. I should have them by the end of the week. I'll also need to take a few more measurements. When would be a good time?"

"Can I call you?" Aleksei asked.

"Of course. I also need you to stop by my office one-day next week to do a tasting and choose the final dishes for the menu."

"What day would you like?" Aleksei asked.

"Let me see," Sheridan said, tapping her tablet. "How about Wednesday at three o'clock?"

"Wednesday it is then," Aleksei agreed. "Miss Harbrook, I still owe you dinner. May I take you out?"

"Sheridan, please" she said.

Aleksei could see the emotions flowing over her features. She wanted to say no but also wanted to impress her client. For a moment, he dared to hope there was some interest in him as a man. He waited quietly, not wanting to influence her further.

"I would be delighted to go to dinner with you. Would you mind if we drove separately? I have an early morning tomorrow and would rather leave from the restaurant," she explained.

She probably played it safe but he admired her for it. "What restaurant would you like to go to?" he asked.

"Well, there is Ruth's Chris, if you want a steak, or there is Spago on Canon Drive."

"It sounds like you prefer Spago. I'll follow you if that is all right," Aleksei said.

"Spago is one of my favorites. I'll wait for you at the end of the drive."

§

Sheridan maneuvered through the streets of Beverly Hills. Christmas wreaths already hung from each street light while tree trunks were wrapped with white and yellow lights.

Daven McCloud had picked up that she preferred Spago. *Amazing*. She also couldn't believe how interested he had seemed to be about the decorating process. When she had observed him at parties before, he always seemed so insincere and flighty, a new starlet on his arm every night. She thought that underneath his lightness was a sad, lonely man. She checked the rearview mirror to make sure he still followed her and saw his shiny red sports car on her tail.

Tonight, he had seemed grounded, confidant, and sincere. He listened to her ideas and came up with a couple of good suggestions of his own. He made her feel valued. It had been such a surprise she hadn't wanted it to end.

She had always thought Daven good looking, but tonight, he seemed even more so. It wasn't just the business suit and haircut either. There was a certain something she couldn't put her finger on. Whatever it was, it drew her. She could have finished their meeting without the dinner with him but she had been so tempted. Then he had waited patiently for her answer.

That was what sold her on the idea. There was no guilt or logical coercion. He waited for her to decide. Now he followed her to her favorite restaurant.

Maybe she had thought him to be a sad, lonely man, because she was a sad, lonely woman. Well not really *sad* but lonely definitely. She had so little time to herself. She always worked, or took care of her mother. Her mother's illness worsened and the doctors were talking about a nursing home.

Sheridan would keep her at home as long as she could. With her career finally taking off, she could afford to hire someone to stay with mom. Tonight, she would be paying overtime but she had scheduled the meeting weeks ago.

She pulled up to the front of the restaurant and the valet opened her door. Daven pulled up behind her and got out. He walked up and offered his arm as a second valet handed him his ticket.

"Shall we?" he asked, looking down at her.

Suddenly, goosebumps broke out on Sheridan's skin. She felt exposed. Daven's eyes turned yellow for a moment. Then they were blue again.

What was that? It must be a reflection from the lights. She nodded and they went inside. Daven asked for a table.

"Mr. McCloud, how nice of you to join us tonight. Would you like your usual table?" The maître de asked. For some reason Daven seemed to hesitate.

"I think a table by the fountain would be nice for a change."

"Of course, Mr. McCloud, right this way."

They were seated where they had a nice view of the ornamental water feature. The area was already festooned with green garland and white lights. After Thanksgiving, the fountain would be covered by a Christmas tree.

So, Daven came here enough to have a special table?

§

Aleksei knew Daven was more of the private room-trysting type. Now that Penny had a hold of him that would probably change. Alek was pretty sure Sheridan would not like Daven's *normal* table. He had generously tipped the maître de when they were seated.

Aleksei and Sheridan each looked at the menu and then each other. Aleksei could almost see Sheridan's curiosity about his friend's normal table.

"I sometimes have business dinners here," he lied. For some reason he didn't want her to think badly of him or Daven. Sheridan raised her eyebrow at him. *She wasn't buying it.*

"What did you decide on?" he asked, changing the subject.

"Oh, I'm going to have the Spago Greek salad. You?" she asked.

"I feel the need for meat. I'm going for the prime rib."

The waiter came for their orders and Aleksei added a bottle of wine.

"So how did you get into the party planning business?" he asked.

Before long, their dinner came. They talked and laughed throughout. Aleksei kept the conversation about Sheridan and wasn't disappointed.

She talked about her mother but he could tell the situation was not a happy one. So, he brought the conversation back to her business. It wasn't long before he found out she loved the color purple and her favorite flower was violets.

He asked her about her favorite party themes. Then what party she wished she could throw. He learned all about her. He loved how animated she got when she talked about her work. As well as telling him one funny story after the other about party disasters. Then how she overcame said disaster, even if it meant giving a refund to the client.

28

Aleksei realized that he liked her. She was a genuinely nice person who loved her job and was good at it. Over after-dinner coffee, she talked about the subtle elegant style she wanted to bring to Daven's party. She had the perfect feel for what *he* wanted. Of course, it was Daven's party and he would have left everything to Sheridan, offering no comment or inspiration. So, whatever the two of them decided would work for Daven.

It was finally time to leave and Aleksei didn't want to let her go.

"I had a wonderful time tonight, Daven."

"I did, too," Aleksei said, walking her to her car.

"I'll call you later in the week and we can schedule our next time to meet," she said, looking up at him. He could happily fall into her beautiful eyes.

"I'll be waiting," he answered.

Then he slowly lowered his lips to hers. He gave her plenty of time to say no but he was so glad she didn't. He kissed her gently and felt her sigh. He slipped his tongue in for a quick caress, but knew that now was not the time, and standing on the street was not the place.

He released her reluctantly and waved as she drove away. His wolf howled its frustration. It wanted her. Aleksei wouldn't play games with Sheridan. If she was his mate the heartmate bond would show itself.

Aleksei got into his car and drove back to Daven's house. When he drove up to the building, he felt his hackles raise. Someone had been snooping around.

He stepped into Shadow, that dimension next to Earth, and investigated the perimeter. Whoever it was had been watching from across the street at first. Aleksei stepped out of Shadow to use his Lycan senses. The man's smell was more pronounced near the front gate, like he had stood in one spot a long time. He obviously climbed over the wall and had come up to the house to check the doors and windows. Aleksei could smell the intruder's scent on the handles and sashes.

Next, he tracked the scent into the garage. Scratches on the lock showed it had been tampered with to get open. The smell was very strong around Daven's Mercedes. Aleksei would check it in the daylight. If he couldn't tell whether it had been tampered with himself, by scent, he'd call out a tow truck and take it to a mechanic.

He Shadow Walked into the foyer, staying in Shadow, while he checked for signs of entry inside. He didn't find anything and after stepping out of Shadow, his wolf didn't sense anyone in the house.

He headed upstairs and undressed, carefully hanging Daven's suit. Then he slipped the big neon orange dog collar over his head and let his wolf come to the surface.

Once he was wolf, he checked the perimeter again. He could smell the man on the other side of the doors and windows but he had not come into the house. At least now, Aleksei had his scent and would recognize it easily. He ran back upstairs and jumped up on the bed, deciding to stay wolf for the night.

He could see himself in the mirror of the dresser. He kind of liked his neon orange collar. It looked good against his black fur. His wolf agreed with him as he circled slowly and laid down to sleep. With his wolf hearing and sense of smell, no one would get in undetected. *Did Sheridan like wolves?*

§

Sheridan kicked herself all the way home. *Why did she let him kiss her? And heaven help her, why did she kiss him back?* Maybe it was the way he had watched her eyes, to see if it was okay. She had *wanted* the kiss, had been thinking about it all through dinner.

She loved the beautiful color of Daven's eyes, like the ocean surrounding a tropical island. For a moment, she imagined that she could see down to his soul.

He had wanted her of that she was sure. She'd been around men enough to feel their interest and sometimes, she seemed able to pick up on other's feelings. She hadn't needed psychic powers to know he wanted her. It radiated

30

off him in waves. She was very much afraid she wanted him as badly.

Luckily it had only been one kiss and not a long one. Though that had been slightly disappointing. *One* kiss, which was good and bad, because she had to work for this man.

Everyone knew you shouldn't mix sex with business. Even though, for a moment, she had wanted Daven McCloud hot, sweaty, and ready for her.

Still, only one small kiss. Sheridan felt her lips carefully. *Would other kisses ever measure up to tonight's kiss?* Lying a little to herself, *surely by the time she had to go back to Daven's house, she would be over one little kiss.*

She pulled into her driveway and parked. All the lights were on in the small ranch house. Sheridan ran inside afraid something was wrong. Mrs. Salazar, the nurse, sat reading in the chair.

"Is everything all right? Why are all the lights on? Is my mother asleep?" Sheridan asked in quick succession.

"Yes, your mother is sleeping. You don't like the lights, you can turn them off. My money please, it's late. Don't forget to add the five extra hours, that's $150.00 more."

Sheridan had planned to have dinner, but not stay out so late.

"All right," Sheridan said. "Who comes tomorrow?"

"My sister, Luisa. She will be here at eight o'clock like you asked," Salazar rattled on as Sheridan wrote out a check and handed it to her.

The nurse folded it crisply in half with determined precision. "Goodnight, Miss Harbrook. It is very late, you should go to sleep," she suggested as she left.

Sheridan went from room to room turning off lights. Finally, she reached her mother's door and peeked in to see her sleeping soundly. She turned off the hall light and walked into her room.

Her bedroom was the smaller of the two but that didn't bother her. It was big enough for a queen size bed and that was all she needed. Sometimes, she would get frustrated with her overly small closet but she got over it.

She liked her family's nice little ranch style home. Occasionally, she wished she had more room to spread out, but since that dream was impossible, she let it go. She got into a pair of cotton pajamas and crawled into bed. Her last thought was of Daven McCloud and how different he had looked tonight. Then, as she drifted off, a vision of a large black wolf wearing a neon orange collar crept into her mind. Sheridan smiled in her sleep.

Chapter Three

The morning brought sunshine and blue skies to Beverly Hills. Aleksei got up and stretched, his wolf tail waving high in the air. Then he got off the bed and did another tour of the perimeter.

There was a small room off the Master bedroom that may have been used as a nursery once upon a time. It could easily be remodeled and reinforced into a safe room and wired with the master control panel for the security cameras and recording devices. If needed, Daven would be able to go into the safe room and observe the intruder with the cameras. A panic button would send an alarm to Isanti, Inc. as well as local law enforcement and emergency services. It would be a start at protecting Daven, but they still needed to find who wanted to kill him and why?

Aleksei went upstairs and changed his form, dressed and headed out to the garage. He climbed underneath the Mercedes's chassis, looking for something wrong or damaged, using his wolf nose to check for the stranger's scent.

He didn't find anything underneath the car but he could smell how the man had circled around the vehicle several times. The doors were locked and the windows up, so maybe the stranger became frustrated and left. Of course, a mechanic should check it over anyway.

Daven's brakes on the sport's car had already been tampered with. Aleksei wasn't going to take the chance that the Mercedes had been tampered with as well. Glancing at Daven's watch, he went back into the house. He had enough time to eat before Shadow Walking to Isanti. First, he needed a shower.

Daven must have remodeled the master bath. It was filled with marble and brushed chrome. Aleksei gazed in appreciation at the large free-standing tub and the glass-enclosed shower. Both fixtures had room for two. The shower even had extra jets that would spray from the sides as well as the top.

Aleksei turned on the shower. The water quickly warmed as he disrobed. Touching the control pad, he directed all the jets to come on. He groaned and leaned closer to the warm water surrounding him.

"I think I need one of these in my apartment."

The need to get back to New Mexico forced Aleksei from the shower's indulgence and into the closet, grabbing Daven's clothes to wear. Since he was going into the office, he put on a pair of business slacks and a shirt and tie. He especially liked the cobalt colored shirt and Jerry Garcia tie. *Too bad Sheridan couldn't see him.* He shook his head at such a silly thought.

Breakfast was next. Entering the kitchen, he checked the cupboards and found a box of cereal. There wasn't any milk in the refrigerator, but he found eggs.

"Daven must eat out all the time," he grumbled.

Aleksei would definitely need to go to the grocery store if he stayed in this house. He finished his scrambled eggs and then found a patch of shadow in the hall. Near the edges the shadow wavered slightly. Slipping his hands inside, he pulled open a door into the Shadow Dimension. Once inside, he visualized his office in New Mexico and all the little details. The ground slipped beneath him, like sand on the beach, and then he looked out at his office as if through a dirty window. Opening another portal, he walked out of the near-Earth dimension and into his work space. He pushed the intercom button on his desk.

"Janet, can you please inform Penny and Daven that I'm back from California?" he asked his secretary.

"Yes, Mr. Sokolov, right away."

Aleksei didn't have long to wait. In minutes Penny and Daven burst into the room.

"Alek, you're okay?" Daven asked.

"Did you find anything?" Penny asked.

Aleksei held up his hand to get their attention.

"Good morning. I love the new bathroom, Daven, and I have to get one of those showers. I found out that someone is definitely watching the house. I didn't see him but my wolf could smell where he'd been. I need the number of your mechanic to make sure the Mercedes wasn't tampered with last night. And I need to borrow Penny."

"What do you mean?" Daven asked, wrapping his arm around Penny's waist.

"I want her to come to the house and help me place the equipment. It's her department and she excels at her job," Aleksei said. Daven clenched his jaw. He didn't like the idea. "If you promise to stay in the house and out of sight you can come too," Aleksei continued. "It should only take the afternoon for Penny and I to find the best placement for the cameras and audio recorders. She can Shadow Walk you both back here or to her parent's house in Montana when we're done."

"I thought you said it would put her in danger to be there," Daven said.

"Penny will be fine. She'll be surrounded by Shadow Walkers and as long as no one sees you while we're there we should be okay. Daven, I don't want anyone to figure out there are two of us. This whole plan will go up in flames if they realize I'm not you. Do you understand?" Aleksei asked.

"Sure, I understand, but if Penny goes then I go. I can't let her go without me," Daven said, rather sheepishly "You'll have to forgive me, this mating thing is all new to me. You're my best friend, but right now it's driving me crazy to know you're in the same room with Penny."

"Think how you're going to feel having her surrounded by Shadow Walkers." Aleksei paused a moment. "They'll try to give you some space but they can't protect either one of you if they don't stay close. If you can't handle this, we can ask Dr. Rick for a sedative for you. Once you're out, Penny can come with me. She'll be back before you wake up. It'll be hard on her leaving you drugged up. It's up to you. Make your decision. I want to get this project done and you safe," Aleksei said.

The first couple of days were the hardest on a newly mated couple. Fights had broken out before when an unmated male got too close to a newly mated pair. Somehow mated males didn't bring about the same response, or at least not as strongly. Daven would feel that Aleksei was a threat.

"I'll come. I'll hide upstairs while you work. I need to get some information off my laptop anyway," Daven said, coolly. Aleksei noticed Daven stayed between him and Penny.

"Look Daven I know you feel a little out of control right now. Remember, I'm your friend. I'm trying to help. Shall we go meet the rest of the team?" Aleksei asked.

"We can do this, Daven," Penny said, placing her hand in his.

Daven swept her aside, letting his friend take the lead. Aleksei knew it was more to keep him in sight then letting him lead. *Would he be this bad when he found his mate?* Aleksei chuckled to himself. *Probably worse.*

"Who's in charge of the installation team, Penny?" he asked.

"My brother, Joe."

"Good," Aleksei said. Joe was good at his job. As Penny's sibling, he wouldn't be a threat to Daven.

Joe? Aleksei sent telepathically.

Here....

I need you to swap out any unmated males on the McCloud project and replace them with mated ones. I've got Penny's new mate with me. He's still a little unstable.

I'll take care of it.

Thanks Joe.

You're the Boss, Aleksei.

Aleksei walked the long way to the elevators taking back hallways. After a quick ride, they stepped out of the elevator into the lobby. Aleksei led Penny and Daven up to the six men standing in the shadows waiting for them.

You have a twin you forgot to mention? Joe asked telepathically.

He's my college buddy, and yes, we raised hell because no one could tell us apart. Aleksei sent telepathically in reply.

Aleksei made introductions. Daven wasn't quite as nervous with these men as he was of Aleksei. The men surrounded the couple, being careful not to touch Penny. They all followed Aleksei into Shadow and out into the foyer of Daven's house.

"Daven upstairs and stay away from the windows." Aleksei ordered his friend. "Penny go with him and get him settled. Then come back downstairs." Daven and Penny ran up the stairs and disappeared.

"Joe, we have the possibility of a watcher, someone was out there last night. Can one of your men check the perimeter?"

"No problem, Boss." One of the men disappeared into Shadow.

"Once we know it's clear," Aleksei said, addressing the rest of the men, "one of you will need to Shadow Walk to the airport and pick up a vehicle and the equipment. The rest of us will start making notes of repairs and figuring placements of equipment. Joe, if you will go with Penny, she'll show you the best camera locations. I think there is a room next to the master bedroom that will work for a safe room and control center. The door will need to be measured as well as wall covering ordered for the walls. A secured phone line will need to be run into the control center as well. Questions?" Aleksei asked, "Good, here comes Penny. Joe, I want three people on her when you go outside. Okay team, let's get to work. Are we clear, Joe?"

"Yes, we appear to be clear. No watcher detected. Don't worry about Penny. We'll keep her safe," Joe said.

"I know you will. I'm heading out to the pool house. I want to see where we can put a camera," Aleksei said, moving toward the back of the house.

He had decided to stay as far away from Penny as he could. It would ease Daven's nerves until he got used to being connected to Penny telepathically.

The rest of the afternoon went quickly. Penny finished her assessment of the property and ordered a few more pieces of equipment to be delivered next day.

The whole team collectively breathed a sigh of relief when Penny Shadow Walked her mate back to New Mexico. They had all gone through the mating process themselves and knew how crazy it could make you feel.

Aleksei was teased by the other men about still being unmated and that soon his turn would come. He took it all good naturedly and thought about Sheridan. *Did she think about him?*

When it was finally time to quit for the night, Aleksei was pleased with all that had been accomplished. There were now sensors on every door and window. Motion detection lights were installed around the perimeter, as well as cameras and audio sensors. There was a brand new electric gate and generator in case of power failure. Not all of the systems were able to record yet and several of the hidden cameras in the house still needed adjusting but Aleksei was sure that by the end of the week the whole project would be finished.

Since he would be sleeping in the master bedroom, he would hear the warning alarm when a camera activated. Even with the system only halfway complete, he felt the perimeter would be hard to penetrate without detection. Whoever the stranger was, he would now have to watch from outside the property line.

Penny, in the course of her work of looking in every corner of the house, noticed the lack of food and had ordered in groceries so Aleksei didn't have to leave the estate. Except for his appointment with Sheridan, he could stay holed up here until Daven and Penny figured out who was behind the accidents.

After Thanksgiving, Penny and Daven could come back to the house when everything was secure. They would still have to be careful. A bullet could come through a window or hit them in the yard. It was up to Daven of course. He could stay in New Mexico or Montana without anyone being the wiser. Aleksei almost hoped they did stay away. He didn't want his friend at risk.

Isanti, Inc. made some inquiries. So far, there were only rumors about Daven becoming CEO. Nothing about any bad blood or disappointed stock holders. It also appeared that Daven's parents' deaths were indeed accidental.

Aleksei forced himself to do another perimeter check. The day caught up to him and his stomach grumbled. He still needed to eat something.

Everything appeared to be clear. So he went into the kitchen and microwaved a boxed meal Penny ordered. He was too tired to cook tonight. He ate quickly and then headed upstairs.

Someone would have to hire a household staff. Isanti would run background checks screening the potential staff. Aleksei really hoped it would be someone else doing the interviews. He didn't want to be involved in hiring Daven's house and grounds keeping.

He also needed to find out who Sheridan would be hiring for the party. There would be servers and bartenders. He didn't know how many. He'd have to call her and ask. He hoped she wouldn't be upset that he would need to do background checks on her staff. If he was lucky, she had already done a party where that was asked of her.

As if thinking of Sheridan brought her into his mind, a vision appeared of her at a party. She wore a lovely gold gown. Her auburn hair was up in the back but curls seemed to be escaping the pins and one fell gently against her cheek, while another fell softly down her neck. She stood in a kitchen directing the food serving staff. Aleksei wanted to run his hand up her bare back and cup the nape of her neck. He could almost feel her soft skin. She shivered as if she felt his hands on her. As quickly as the vision came, it was gone, leaving Aleksei wanting more.

§

Sheridan had done it again. The Biltmore Autumn Gala had gone off without a hitch. The decorations were perfect and complimented the wooden paneling and old world style of the ballroom.

The hotel management had complimented her over and over again and she now had a nice big deposit in the bank. She had worn her gold evening gown but had forgotten a coat. As she waited for the valet to bring up her car, she shivered in the cool California evening air.

The day had started off horribly when her mother fell. Sheridan called the paramedics, and then followed the ambulance to the hospital. The doctor kept pushing for a nursing home and Sheridan didn't want to face or be forced into that decision yet. The only good thing about all this was she wasn't paying Mrs. Salazar overtime tonight. The attendant drove up and held her car door open for her. She climbed in.

Sheridan got on the freeway and headed the car toward home all the while worrying about her mother. She had hoped that by working less hours and going into the office later, she would be able to give her mother the time and attention she needed.

It didn't seem to be working. Now, during the holiday party season, Sheridan had to work late into the night or early morning nearly every day. And after this last accident, she was very afraid that the doctor was right. She should put her mom someplace where she had 24-hour care.

It wasn't her mother who resisted but Sheridan herself. How could she turn her mother out of her own house? Her mother's fall today confirmed that her physical wellbeing was at stake. Mom even told her there needed to be a change.

Sheridan realized suddenly that tears were pouring down her face. Luckily, the Los Angeles freeways weren't as crowded at this hour. She finally pulled into her own driveway and looked at the ranch style home where she'd grown up.

She had forgotten to leave a light on and the house looked dark and sad. Climbing out of the car seemed like a chore but she made it into the empty house. Everything seemed so quiet.

Sheridan thought of Daven being all alone in his *big* house. Was he lonely? She could picture him sleeping with his long black eyelashes resting closed against his cheek and his blond hair mussed. He looked younger when he slept, not as focused, or confidant, but relaxed. She watched as his eyes opened, sleepy and warm as he looked at her.

Do you come to me in my dreams, Sherry? She heard in her mind.

Sheridan gasped. *What just happened? Had she really heard Daven's voice in her head?*

She was exhausted. "I'm probably only imagining things."

She shook her head and walked down the hall to her room. Pulling off her clothes and pulling on pajamas, she climbed under the covers. Visiting hours started at nine at the hospital and she wanted to be there for her mom.

Chapter Four

Aleksei woke up smiling, remembering a dream of Sheridan coming to him. He stretched and wished he didn't have to get up so early. Joe and his crew would be showing up and he needed to call Daven's mechanic today to check on the Mercedes. He smiled again when he remembered Daven's shower and jumped out of bed. He wanted to spend every possible minute under the water jets.

He had finished dressing when he felt Joe's mental call.

Hey, Boss. Ready for company?

Come on ahead and let's get this thing finished.

Bad news, the door for the safe room won't be ready until tomorrow. We can focus on the other projects.

Do what you can. I'll be down in five, sent Aleksei and then he cut the link.

Aleksei walked downstairs in time to see Joe and his team step through Shadow. It always gave him a thrill to see how the shadows in the room would seem to come together and then a man would step out. Of course, if there were no shadows then a person couldn't step out, so they all had to be careful not to be caught in bright light during transfer. Aleksei shook hands with Joe and greeted the other members of the team.

"There's coffee in the kitchen. Do a perimeter check and then let's get to work," Aleksei said.

"Sure thing, Boss," Joe answered.

Aleksei went into Daven's office and sat at the desk. He needed to call the mechanic and for some reason he wanted to call Sheridan. The mechanic promised to come for the car this morning. When Aleksei pulled up

Sheridan's business information, he found himself hesitating. He didn't want to appear impatient. She had said she would call to come show him samples. He thought about it for a while and decided to risk it. The phone rang several times.

"Enchanted Evenings, this is Sara, how may I help you?"

"Sara, this is Daven McCloud, may I speak to Miss Harbrook?"

"I'm sorry, Mr. McCloud, but Sheridan is out of the office. She isn't expected in until late this afternoon. May I have her call you?"

Aleksei knew something wasn't right in Sheridan's life. The feeling told him he should be worried.

"That would be fine. Uh, I know this is personal but is Sheridan's mother all right?"

"Oh, you know about the fall? She broke her hip but Sheridan said she would be okay."

"Thank you for telling me. Is she at Cedars-Sinai? I'd like to send flowers."

"Yes, the room number is 1204."

"Thank you, Sara."

"Thank you, Mr. McCloud. I'll be sure to tell Sheridan you called."

Aleksei called Janet to send the flowers but he wondered how Sheridan was holding up. He hoped she was doing okay. He missed her warm smile.

"Janet, I need flowers sent to Sheridan Harbrook's mother at Cedar-Sinai Medical Center, room 1204. Make sure the card says Daven McCloud. Also send a bouquet of violets to Miss Sheridan Harbrook at her office. Have the card say 'thinking of you, Daven.' Thanks, Janet," Aleksei said and hung up.

He growled. Signing the cards with Daven's name seemed wrong. His wolf fussed in his head. The need to lie bothered him. His wolf knew Aleksei wanted Sheridan to know the flowers were from him. Of course, Sheridan thought he was Daven, so why did his heart beat so hard and his stomach feel tied in knots? Aleksei sighed and went out to receive the perimeter check report and help with the installation.

He found Joe upstairs working in the control room. Aleksei grimaced. He hadn't bothered to make the bed.

"You were right about your watcher. Thunderhoof found evidence of someone standing across the street. Unfortunately, none of the cameras are pointed in that direction, so we don't have a visual on him," Joe reported.

"Can we set up the perimeter cameras to scan outside the mansion grounds? It would really help to know who we're dealing with here."

"I'll get one of the guys working on it. The computer systems should be up and on line today. You'll be able to review them in the morning to see if this guy shows up tonight. The in-house cameras probably won't be up until tomorrow."

"Okay, let's get it done. A mechanic from Mercedes-Benz Beverly Hills will be coming to tow Daven's Mercedes. Let him in for the car but don't leave him alone. Everyone is suspect until we know who we're dealing with," Aleksei said.

"I'll inform the guys working on the front gate."

Aleksei ran his hands through his hair. If he could figure out who the threat was he could tell Sheridan the truth. He *needed* to tell her for his own wellbeing.

The day passed quickly and Aleksei worked on connecting the in-house cameras when the phone rang. He could see on the caller ID that it was Sheridan calling.

"Hi, I called to let you know the flowers are beautiful. My mother was especially touched, and I have no idea where you had to go to order fresh violets but thank you so much," Sheridan gushed over the phone.

"I'm glad you like them, Sherry. I worried about you when Sara told me the news. Are you all right?"

§

Sheridan started talking and suddenly it all flowed out. Her mother's illness and needing to put her in a nursing

45

home and how guilty she felt. Sheridan didn't know why she told Daven all her woes. Maybe it was because he had called her Sherry in her dream.

When the flowers had been delivered to her mother's room they had both been surprised. Her mother grilled her for information and didn't accept Sheridan's explanation of Daven being a client.

Then, when she had gotten to her office and saw the teacup full of violets waiting for her, tears had come to her eyes. She remembered telling Daven violets were her favorite flower but didn't expect him to remember. The fact that he did, touched her heart and told her he really listened. Daven McCloud was someone she could really like. She feared he might turn into someone she could *more* than like.

Sheridan hadn't been on a real date since she graduated from college. Her mother had been ill even then. When her father died, she had stopped thinking of having a romantic relationship. Daven changed all that. But with her mother in the hospital and the holidays before her.... She stopped herself. The timing was terrible. She had too much on her plate right now. It didn't stop her from dreaming but right now, she didn't have time for anything else.

"When can I see the samples? I'm not trying to rush you but I'm a little excited," Aleksei asked.

"I have a party tomorrow night and I don't usually work on Sundays, but if you wish, I can stop by around six o'clock Sunday evening. I'll show you the samples and we can talk some more about placement."

"That sounds great. I'll fix dinner. I know you like pasta. You can bring the wine," Aleksei said.

Sheridan laughed. "That sounds great, dinner it is."

Sheridan hung up the phone and wondered if she had made the right decision. She had promised to meet him for dinner before so it would seem strange if she refused now. It didn't have to *mean* anything. It was a business dinner like the last one. But it already did mean something.

§

Aleksei smiled as he hung up and looked forward to seeing Sheridan again. He could make a mean Alfredo sauce and would have all the ingredients stocked before Sunday. Now, if he could just let her know his real name. It grated on his nerves when she called him Daven. Aleksei sighed and got back to work. Next week was Thanksgiving and they would soon run out of time before the party. *Did Daven and Penny find anything?*

He'd call them tonight, he decided as he finished the install on the camera in the dining room. He was especially proud of that one. There was a rosette on the wall and they had placed the lens dead center in the rosette. No one would notice it if they didn't know it was there. There were cameras in each of the downstairs rooms but the one in the dining room was the only one hooked up. The rest of the crew would come in and finish hooking up the other cameras tomorrow. He could have finished tonight if he worked until the early hours but there really wasn't a rush.

§

Aleksei woke-up on Sunday morning to a bright sunny day with blue skies. He started to understand why everyone loved California. He couldn't wait for Sheridan to come for dinner tonight. He had all the ingredients for his Alfredo sauce as well as the pasta and French bread.

He checked the cameras from the night before. It seemed as if the watcher had disappeared, which made Aleksei nervous. He doubted that whoever it was had given up. He hadn't left the estate for the last week and now wondered if it was safe to do so. The security system was in place and finished. A Shadow Walker would be in the control center the night of the party to monitor all systems, as well as others on the grounds. For now, it was the best he could do.

Tonight, he would ask for a list of Sheridan's staff so the background checks could be completed. Daven had already given Isanti, Inc. a copy of the guest list. Maybe he could enjoy his dinner tonight without too much worry.

Aleksei had been missing a lot of time at work and decided to Shadow Walk back to New Mexico. He would be back in time to fix dinner. He walked into the closet and then into Shadow.

When Aleksei Shadow Walked into his office, Daven stood waiting. Walking around his desk, Alek sat down before his friend decided to speak.

"I hoped you would be here," Daven said. "I would like to ask you to be my best man. Penny and I want to get married as soon as possible. We Shadow Walked into New York City yesterday and went to Tiffany's to buy a ring," Daven explained.

"Congratulations, Daven, it would be my honor to be your best man. When are you planning the ceremony?" Aleksei asked.

"Penny wants it to be December 1st. I don't have any family left and you're the only one that matters to me, so we're going to have the ceremony at your family compound in Montana."

"That sound's great. But have you found anything out about who might want to kill you?" Aleksei asked, suddenly irritated with Daven and his lack of focus on the problem at hand.

All this time he was in California, making himself a target, while Daven planned a wedding and enjoyed his mate. When would they find their attempted murderer?

"We're pretty sure it's someone on the board. Penny and I have been searching computer files but so far no luck."

"Who is the CEO right now?"

"Sylvester Adams, but he's seventy years old and wants to retire. He probably wishes I'd take over now instead of after the New Year. It's not him. No, something else is going on. I'm just not sure what."

"What about voting blocks, have you checked old board meeting minutes to see if there is a pattern to the voting?"

"That was one of the first places I looked." Daven rubbed his neck. "I know you're getting tired of pretending to be me, but is it so bad? If you wanted to you could Shadow Walk anywhere in the world."

"Yeah, all alone, that sounds fun doesn't it," Aleksei grumbled.

Was that why he was irritated, because he was lonely? Or was he jealous of his friend finding his mate? Aleksei hoped he wasn't that shallow but at the moment he felt a little used.

"Look Daven, I'm sorry for being such a grouch. I'm really happy for you and Penny. When do you think you'll want to move back in?"

"I'm not sure, probably not until the party December 20th. I would like to introduce my new bride to the board members that night."

"Then you better figure out who we're looking for. I know you don't want to take a chance with Penny," Aleksei reminded his friend.

"Don't worry, I remember. How are the party plans going with Sheridan Harbrook?" Daven asked.

"They're going well. I'm meeting with her this evening to pick the color scheme and make the final decisions on where exactly we are placing the trees and garland."

"Wow, you don't have to go to all that trouble. Just tell her to take care of it. I'm sure all her other clients do."

"It's not any trouble. In fact, it seems to be the highlight of my week," Aleksei admitted.

"You like her."

"I do. She's warm, and fun to be with, and really enjoys her job. It can be contagious."

"Is that it? Remember, I know you. Your best friend. Sounds like something else."

"Okay, maybe there is something there. You know about the mating bond. I won't play with Sheridan's affections. If there is no bond then she stays just a friend. Besides, she thinks I'm you," Aleksei said.

"Ah, and you hate that don't you. Don't look at me like that. You hated it in college, too. This is a little different. She hasn't seen the two of us together. We could test her, like we used to in college."

"You do know how infantile that was? It doesn't matter if she's not my mate and if she is then she'll never have trouble telling us apart. So, for now, leave it," Aleksei said.

"If you say so. Have fun with her tonight. Maybe you'll know more after your dinner."

"Go away and let me get some work done. Figure out who our culprit is, and I'll let you test Sheridan, if Penny lets you," Aleksei said, waving his friend to the door.

§

Aleksei was in a good mood as he Shadow Walked back to Daven's estate in California. He had been able to catch up on most of his work and even had time to call and chat with his mother. His two twin sisters' birthday fell on Thanksgiving this year. The whole family would get together. Aleksei looked forward to seeing everyone.

They might even have snow and Aleksei loved the white stuff. He grew up in Montana where the winter brought lots of it. One of his favorite things to do was go wolf and play and romp in the powder. Did Sheridan like snow? Maybe tonight he'd find out.

Aleksei went for a swim in the pool before he showered and dressed for dinner. That hour time difference between California and Albuquerque sure came in handy. He headed into the kitchen to start cooking. While the sauce warmed, he set the table in the kitchen, and fixed a salad. He wouldn't start the linguine until Sheridan arrived.

He went into the front room to find some appropriate music for dinner when the buzzer on the front gate rang. He rushed back into the kitchen and dialed the gate number. As soon as he heard Sheridan's voice over the intercom, he put in the code that allowed the gate to open. Then he started the water boiling for the pasta before going to greet her.

§

Sheridan was a little nervous about meeting with Daven tonight. She had been thinking of their appointment almost like it was a date, which was ridiculous. This was business after all.

Her mother was finally home from the hospital but being unable to walk, Sheridan had been forced to hire twenty-four-hour nursing care. She liked the new nurses but the doctor, nurses, and her mother all seemed to be ganging up on her about the nursing home. It would be more affordable with Medicare helping and her mother would have twenty-four-hour care. *Maybe after the holidays.*

When her mother said she wanted Sheridan to be free to find a husband, that had really hurt. If Sheridan was honest, she would admit she wanted a relationship. Being her mother's caregiver was a lot of work and sometimes she wished someone would *care* for her. She worked or stayed home with her mother. She only went to parties she contracted. She saw couples, arm-in-arm, and wished that she wasn't so alone.

When Daven sent the violets, she realized no one had given her a "just because" gift for the last three years. What a staggering thought. Three years. She loved her mother and hated the idea of turning her care over to strangers. *Had she become a control freak or codependent along the way? Was she being a good daughter by keeping her mother with her?*

Sheridan drove up to Daven's estate and saw the new gate and call system. She pressed the button.

"Hello?"

"Hi, Daven. It's me, Sheridan Harbrook."

"Come right in," came over the speaker, and then the gate moved off to the side.

Sheridan pulled up to the front door. She could see in her rearview mirror that the gate closed her in. Why had Daven suddenly become so security conscious? Had something happened?

She picked up her box of samples, the bottle of wine, and walked up to the door. She reached for the bell when the door opened and Daven stepped out.

"Here, let me help you," he said, taking the box from her hands. "Dinner is almost ready. Let's go into the kitchen."

Sheridan followed him inside and immediately smelled something wonderful. Daven put down her box on the counter.

"I see you brought wine. Should we open it?"

"Please do," Sheridan said, handing him the bottle.

She liked looking at him and the way he moved with sureness and confidence. He opened the wine and poured them each a glass.

His eyes seemed to see so much, taking in everything. But then he would focus all of his attention on her, making her feel crucial to his existence. He handed her a crystal wine glass and the aroma of berries and cherries filled her senses.

Daven's blond hair seemed to be a little damp like he had showered recently. Not his usual model made-up look. Sheridan liked it.

He added the pasta to the boiling water. Sheridan sipped her wine. They made small talk while he cooked. The scene seemed so intimate somehow, with just the two of them and the smells of good food.

Chapter Five

When Aleksei opened the door and saw Sheridan, his wolf jumped to the surface and he wanted to pull her into his arms. She wore an emerald green silk shirt and a cream-colored skirt. Her hair seemed to be hiding flames in its depths and he found himself reaching for it.

Instead, he took the box from her and brought her into the kitchen. Now he tried to hide the bulge in his pants by staying behind the counter. He probably rambled on about something but couldn't seem to help himself. Taking deep breaths to steady his nerves, he dared to look at her. He didn't see confusion or amusement. She seemed completely at ease sipping her wine. Maybe she hadn't noticed the rambling speech.

The timer rang on the stove and he set about draining the pasta and putting it in a bowl. Then with one last stir, he poured the alfredo sauce over the top and gave it a toss with the pasta server.

"Dinner is ready. If you'll grab the wine, I'll carry this over to the table. Do you like olive oil and herb dressing for your salad? There might be something else in the refrigerator if you don't."

"That dressing sounds delicious."

Aleksei set the food on the table and then sat down. If he could just relax a little, he might be able to get through dinner.

Soon, they were talking and laughing like they had the last time they were together. Aleksei found that Sheridan loved the snow but had never lived in that kind of weather. He wished he could share a winter wonderland with her. After dinner, Aleksei served up sherbet for dessert and started coffee for later.

After he asked about her mother, Sheridan shared how conflicted she was about what was really best for her. Aleksei could understand how painful these decisions could be for a child to make for a parent. It hurt to see the usually warm and funny woman he knew become so quiet and unsure.

"I'm sorry to be spilling my guts here," Sheridan admitted "You seem to be the only person who actually listens. Everyone else is ready to give me their opinion but never really listens to what I say."

"I can see how hard this is on you. Please call me anytime you need to spill your guts," Aleksei teased. Sheridan's smile reappeared.

The conversation finally turned to the party. Sheridan brought the box over to the table to show him the samples. She had put together two different looks. One was gold ribbon with gold, cream, and burgundy ornaments, the other, green and red plaid ribbon with green, red, and cream ornaments.

Aleksei liked the first combination better. It seemed richer to him somehow. They got up and walked around the different rooms a second time and except for a couple of small details, they both agreed with the original placement. They had gone back into the kitchen for a second cup of coffee when Sheridan surprised him by asking about the new gate and security system.

"Did something happen that you needed the upgraded system?" she asked.

"Actually, there have been a couple of strange accidents. Which reminds me, I hope you don't mind but I'll need to have background checks done on any staff you plan to use for the party. Will you be hiring a bartender for this party or is that up to me?"

"Normally I handle the food not the beverages. I know a number of good services if you need help finding someone."

"If I do, I'll call you."

"I'll have the list of staff ready for you on Wednesday at the tasting. Are you still available to come into the office at three?" Sheridan asked.

"Yes, that will be fine."

"The first delivery of ornaments should be arriving the first week of December. When do you want set up to begin?"

"I have a wedding to attend on the first but later that week should be fine. How long does it take?" he asked.

"Usually, a couple of days. How about Thursday and Friday of that week, around ten o'clock?"

"That sounds perfect," Aleksei said, as he gazed into her golden hazel eyes.

Sheridan seemed to become flustered and soon gathered up her things to go. Aleksei glanced at the clock. It was after ten. *Where had the time gone?*

He walked her out to the car and held her door for her. She lowered the driver's side window. She turned toward him and hesitated. Aleksei couldn't help but steal a kiss. Sheridan's lips were as soft as he remembered. He ran his tongue over her lower lip. Sheridan opened her mouth and their tongues tangled. He let her do a little exploring before taking possession of the kiss.

Abruptly, the outside perimeter lights turned on. Aleksei pulled back from Sheridan and glanced around the front yard. *Someone is trying to get in.* He sent a telepathic call for help.

"What is it?" Sheridan asked.

"I think we have an unwanted guest," Aleksei said, and sighed.

Joe and two others appeared out of the darkness and ran to his side.

"Joe, can you please escort Sheridan back to her house? Don't worry, Sherry, I'll see you on Wednesday like we planned. This is Joe, he's going to ride home with you and keep you safe."

"Daven?"

"Sherry, please trust me. I'll explain later."

One of the other men covered his back, while the third had already gone back into Shadow to search out the intruder.

"We need to get you in the house, sir. Right now, you're a sitting duck."

§

Sheridan realized these men were professionals. There was some kind of threat. Keeping Daven outside endangered him. The man called Joe climbed in the passenger seat of her car.

"If you'll go ahead and start the engine, miss, we'll get you out of here," Joe said.

Sheridan was relieved to see Daven going back in the house. She turned on the ignition and pulled the car around the driveway toward the gate.

"If you would put up the window and lock the doors," Joe advised.

Sheridan fumbled with the controls and saw the gate moving to the side. She drove out into the night.

§

Make sure you aren't followed. I don't want to lead anyone to Sheridan's door, Aleksei sent telepathically to Joe.

Roger. It looks clear but we'll take a detour anyway, Joe answered.

"Miss Harbrook, when you see a well-lit gas station please pull over?"

"Can I ask why?"

"There are a couple of reasons, actually. First, if someone is following us, I want them to see I'm not Mr. McCloud. Secondly, I'm going to drive. Don't worry, these are precautionary measures."

"Is Daven in danger? Shouldn't we be calling the police?"

"I'm sure he's fine, miss. The new security system has an automatic alarm. There is really no need to worry. There's a gas station up ahead. How much gas do you have? I'll be happy to pay for a fill-up."

"I'm only down a half tank but please do what you think is best."

§

Sheridan watched as Joe filled up the tank. She dutifully moved to the passenger seat and put on her seat belt. She felt a little overwhelmed and tears gathered.

She closed her eyes and somehow could see Daven looking at her. As if they were together in a dream, he pulled her into his arms and held her close.

Don't cry, Sherry. Everything is going to be all right. Trust Joe to get you home.

§

Joe opened the door and got in. He could see that Sheridan's eyes looked wet with tears.

"You're all filled up," he announced cheerfully. "Where would you like to go for a ride?"

"Please, take me home."

"Oh, I will. I just need to know we aren't being followed first. Tell you what, you relax and let me handle things. I'll have you home in a jiffy."

Sheridan decided to do just that. She laid her head back and shut her eyes.

Joe carefully drove first down to Los Angeles, then out to Culver City, and then back to Beverly Hills. For a while, he thought they might have a tail but the car finally stopped following them. They were clear. He looked over at Sheridan as she slept. Aleksei had found a real beauty. He had heard the rumors that Sheridan might be his mate. So far, there was no heartmate bond and until there was, no one really knew. He finally pulled into Sheridan's driveway. It was after midnight. Joe felt bad that it had taken so long but it was important to be safe. He got out and walked around the car and opened the passenger door.

"Miss Harbrook, you're home. Let's get you inside," Joe said.

§

Sheridan came awake and rubbed her eyes. Joe offered his hand, and she grabbed her purse, and then allowed him to help her. He escorted her to the door, and waited until she had it open before he turned to leave.

"Wait, shouldn't I call you a cab?" she asked him.

"That's okay, miss, I have my own way back. You have a nice evening now. I'll let the Boss know you're home."

"Thank you, Joe. Please take good care of Daven."

"We will, miss," Joe said, and then he walked away.

§

Aleksei went straight upstairs and into the control room. His Shadow Walker guard took up a position at the door where he could see down the hall.

A row of red lights on the computer console indicated where the perimeter had been breached. He turned on the recorders and saw a man scale the wall on the south side. He dressed all in black and wore a black ski mask. When the lights came on and the cameras started turning, the man seemed to panic and quickly left the same way he came in.

Aleksei needed to have Daven look at this picture and see if he recognized the intruder. If he had been a professional hit man, he wouldn't have been surprised with the lights and cameras. He didn't seem to be carrying a weapon that could be seen. Aleksei wasn't sure what to make of it. He sent a telepathic call to Penny.

I need you to bring Daven through Shadow and to the control room. He needs to look at this footage and see if he recognizes this guy.

We'll be there in ten minutes. We have to...uh...get dressed.

Aleksei was pretty sure he interrupted something between Daven and his mate but at the moment felt no remorse.

Then he felt Sheridan and the wave of fear and worry that threatened to swallow her whole. He reached for her telepathically, held her and comforted her. She needed to trust Joe to get her home safe.

Then the feeling disappeared and Aleksei wasn't sure if they had really connected telepathically or not. The second Shadow Walker appeared in the room.

"I didn't find anything, sir. He must have run when the lights came on. Definitely not a professional. Can we check the camera that covers the street on that side? Maybe we can catch a picture of the car he drove."

"Good idea, have we met? I'm sorry to say I don't know everyone in security," Aleksei admitted.

"No problem, sir, we're the Redtree twins, I'm Ben, and your guard is my brother, Brad. When Joe yelled, we came running."

"Ben go ahead and check that outside camera. Brad, Penny and her mate should be arriving anytime. So, don't be surprised."

"Got it, Boss," Brad answered.

Ben worked the computer console like a pro. He found the picture of a dark sedan leaving the area in a hurry. The license plate appeared to be covered in dirt and grime.

"Give me a few minutes. I'll see if I can get those numbers so we can read them," Ben said.

"Can you work on a close up of our intruder?" Aleksei asked.

"Let me pull up another program."

Just then, Penny and Daven stepped through Shadow and into the room. Daven's arm rested possessively around Penny's waist. Aleksei backed up to give them more room. Daven saw the gesture and smiled.

"It's okay, Alek, I know you're not a threat. Everything seems to have settled. I'll always be possessive, but I don't have the out of control feelings of jealousy I did earlier. Talk about a caveman trip," Daven said, shaking his head.

They hugged warmly. Penny went over to the computer and started working with Ben.

It took a while but Ben discovered the license plate number. Penny called the security office at Isanti to run it. They were still working on the face of the intruder, when Joe appeared in the room.

"Sheridan is home safe and sound and told me to take good care of you, Boss."

"Thanks, Joe, that makes me feel better. Any problems?" Aleksei asked.

"No, I thought we had a tail for a while but either I was wrong or the guy gave up. It was a black sedan, California license plate SGT-364."

"That's the number we got too, you were definitely followed. I wonder why he gave up?" Penny said.

"I had Sheridan stop at a gas station and made myself very visible. He knew he wasn't following Daven. He was probably curious but not so much he wanted to follow us around. He gave up and turned off in Culver City," Joe reported.

"If you got his plate number, he could have gotten Sheridan's. Damn, I didn't think of that. I hope we're not endangering her," Aleksei said, frowning.

"If it's someone from the board then they already know Sheridan is the party planner for the board Christmas Party. I doubt she's in any kind of danger," Daven said.

Aleksei clenched his jaw. Sheridan must stay safe, even if it meant he guarded her himself.

"We can have security do sweeps by her house," Joe offered.

"Make sure someone is on her twenty-four seven, at least until we figure out who this guy is," Aleksei said.

"I'll get a team assigned to her right now," Joe said, picking up the phone.

"How's the close up on the man's face coming, Ben?" Aleksei asked.

"I think it's as clear as I can get it. What do you think? Anyone recognize this guy?" Ben asked.

Aleksei, Daven, Joe, and Penny all stared at the photo. There really wasn't much to see. The man wore a black ski mask, and except for his dark eyes, his face was invisible.

"All I can see here is he has brown eyes but he must be a fairly young man to be climbing brick walls," Daven said.

"Unless that's his hobby. If you stay in shape you can climb quite a while," Aleksei said.

"So, we're looking for someone who climbs for a hobby or is physically able to do so, that has to cut your list down," Joe said.

"The problem is all the board members are getting up there in age. I don't think any of them are physically able to climb," Daven said.

"Then you need to look at family members or we're dealing with a hired hand. Penny, what did they find on the license plate?" Aleksei asked.

"They said it's a rental from a budget rent a car in Culver City. I have the address of the franchise."

"Joe, you and I will go ask some questions tomorrow. Maybe see if we can tap into their security cameras. For now, let's call it a night. Thanks for the help, Ben and Brad. Ben, I like what you were able to accomplish tonight. If Joe feels good about it, I'd like you to work the control center the night of Daven's party," Aleksei said.

Everyone turned to look at Joe to see what he would say. Ben and Brad were young but they were quick learners. Ben seemed to be into the technical aspect of security where Brad seemed to be more the hands-on kind.

"That sounds fine with me. I'll pick the rest of the team for the evening. Brad you'll be on perimeter," Joe said.

"Okay, everyone go home, I don't know about you but we should all get some sleep. Joe, I'll see you tomorrow. Penny and Daven, call me if you figure anything out. Goodnight everyone," Aleksei said, releasing the team.

He really wanted them all to go so he could think about this evening. Aleksei walked into the master bedroom and started to strip. He'd take a little run around the perimeter in wolf form and see what he could pick up. He put on the neon orange collar and shifted into his wolf.

Aleksei sniffed the air and headed to the south side of the property. He had to stand on his back feet and reach up his front paws against the brick wall to get a good smell, the same scent as before. What did the man intend this time? Was he snooping or had he planned some other kind of mischief?

Aleksei didn't get that metallic oil smell that signaled a gun, so the man had not intended to shoot Daven. Whatever he had planned had been cancelled when the intruder panicked. Aleksei hoped that the added security would keep the man from trying again.

He continued along the wall and around to the east side of the property. The wall turned into a chain link fence, because of the steepness of the mountain behind the property. Penny had placed motion detectors that would trigger the cameras up here. Someone would have to be really desperate to try to come in this way. He sniffed the ground and only smelled Penny and the installation team. He could smell some wild animals as well. There were squirrels and a rabbit for sure on that mountain.

Everything seemed secure so he continued his trek. The north and west sides had a brick wall like the south side. Aleksei didn't pick up anything, he checked around the garage, which had been made secure with electric doors and a keypad entry on the side, and found nothing unusual there as well.

The stars were out and the night quiet. Aleksei let his wolf go and he ran. He flew around the front of the house. Jumping the hedge, he ran past the pool house. Faster and faster, he pushed himself until he stood back where he started. His tongue hung out and he panted but it had felt good to run.

He could forget everything for a moment and just be. He went back to the master bedroom and jumped on the bed. Resting his head on his paws, he sighed.

§

Wednesday was finally here, and Sheridan didn't know whether to celebrate or make a run for it. She was finally going to see Daven again. She had wanted to call and make sure he was okay but hadn't wanted to intrude. They were still just business associates. Two kisses did not make a relationship. She could wish it was more but if she was truthful with herself, she had to admit that at the most it could be the beginning of a friendship. Two weeks ago, she would have been amazed to think she and Daven McCloud could have that much. She had misjudged him, underneath he wasn't anything like what she thought he would be.

Sheridan dressed with their meeting in mind. She wore a cream-colored silk blouse over a burgundy skirt and found shoes to match the skirt. The high heels helped show off her toned legs. She had worn her hair down. For some reason, she thought Daven liked it that way.

The prepared food samples were laid out on a set of trays when three o'clock arrived. Sara manned the phones so Sheridan, and her cook, Jeffrey, could make up the samples without interruption. Jeffrey teased her about being nervous about the appointment. Sheridan couldn't hide it from her friends. They had been working together for a couple of years now and they were more than just her staff. Jeffrey's little sister, Joanna, a USC undergrad studying design, helped out as a server when they needed an extra hand and Joanna often had a friend who could help out for some extra cash. Sheridan hoped to hire Joanna full time when she graduated.

Just before three, Sheridan went into the bathroom to freshen up. She just got back to her desk, when Sara called to let her know Daven had arrived. She nervously brushed at her skirt and then walked out into the entry and waiting area. Daven leaned confidently against the counter watching as she approached. He wore a navy-blue suit and a blue and silver tie. *He looks good enough to eat.*

She smiled a little nervously not really certain how to greet him. He smiled back. *Women must line up to see that smile.* It certainly worked on her. Sheridan wanted to throw herself into his arms and beg him to make love to her. As if he knew what she thought, his eyes turned a darker blue. Then for a second, they flashed golden. If Sheridan had not been staring so blatantly, she would have missed it. As it was, it turned her on even more.

§

Aleksei found himself smiling in real pleasure. Just seeing Sheridan made him happy. Then he saw the look in her hazel eyes and knew she wanted him. His wolf stirred. He could smell her arousal, mixed with her violet perfume. Sheridan wanting him was a potent aphrodisiac. He moved closer to her and cupped her cheek.

"Sherry, I missed you," he said, quietly.

"I missed you too, Daven."

As if Sheridan had thrown cold water on him hearing Daven's name on her lips killed his passion. It was silly to feel hurt but it didn't stop the pain. Aleksei lowered his hand and stepped back. He saw the confusion on Sheridan's face and feared he had hurt her as well. Aleksei wasn't any closer to finding Daven's killer and couldn't risk telling her the truth but he wanted to. Continuing this farce with her became harder every day.

Joe went and checked on the car rental. No one was surprised to find out the car had been stolen from the lot that night. It had been found abandoned in downtown Los Angeles. No fingerprints had been discovered, which meant no leads. Whoever was behind this knew how to cover their tracks.

Daven and Penny couldn't find a motive. It looked like the company would be declaring bankruptcy if Daven didn't step in and save it. *Why would someone want to kill the golden goose?*

Aleksei realized that Sheridan had said something and now walked away. She paused and looked at him expectantly.

"Are you coming?" she asked.

"I'm sorry, I was thinking about something," Aleksei said, as he followed her across the entry and down the hall to a small room. Pictures of different appetizers decorated the walls. *This must be the tasting room.* Sheridan sat at a table and motioned for Aleksei to join her.

"I hope you like the selection we picked out for you," she said, all business now. Aleksei wondered if it was because of his withdrawal or something else.

"This is Jeffrey, my assistant," she said, as a tall, thin man wearing a chef's hat placed a tray of food on the table.

Aleksei nodded a greeting and was surprised when the man winked at him.

"Sheridan worked on these goodies all morning. You had her in quite a dither," Jeffrey said.

"Did I?" Aleksei asked, looking at Sheridan. He noticed her blushing. She glanced away.

"Well, I'll let you two get on with it," Jeffrey said, winking again as he left the room.

Was Sheridan's assistant trying to set them up? *What was all the winking about?* He looked at Sheridan again and found her pulling out a tablet to take notes. She didn't seem to be in a dither and except for the earlier blush was all business.

"Shall we begin? This first piece is a bacon wrapped water chestnut," she said, pushing the tray toward him.

Aleksei dutifully tasted each offering. There were a couple he liked more than others, like the spinach and cheese in puff pastry. Everything tasted great and seemed acceptable for the party. There were also different cakes to taste. They chose a white cake with amaretto filling and a chocolate cake with white chocolate mousse filling.

After the tasting, Sheridan took him to her office to finish the details. She filled out a formal contract and they both signed, Aleksei signing Daven's name. Then Aleksei gave her Daven's credit card for the deposit. Sheridan handed him a sheet with her staff's personal information so he could run the background checks and then set a time to come over to start the decorating after the first of December.

Then she stood and shook Aleksei's hand. He suddenly realized she wanted him to leave. She smiled but her eyes had lost their warmth. He didn't release her hand and pulled her into his arms. He held her gently and patted her on the back.

"Sheridan, please forgive me if I've said or done something to hurt you. I don't want to cause you any pain."

"I don't understand you. What do you want from me?" Sheridan asked, her voice a bit wobbly. "One minute you seem to want me and the next you turn away."

"I do want you, Sherry, more than I thought could be possible. I can't make a commitment to you right now. Things aren't safe around me and I can't guarantee your safety if someone knows how I feel about you," Aleksei said, knowing he wasn't making things better.

"What *do* you feel about me?" Sheridan asked.

"I like you. I like your passion and enthusiasm. Seeing you makes me happy," Aleksei said, knowing he only admitted to the tip of the iceberg.

"Seeing you makes me happy, too," she answered quietly, as she pulled away from him.

§

Sheridan could see the torment on his face and wanted more than anything to ease it.

"It's okay, Daven. I'll be here when you want me. I'm not going anywhere."

Sheridan saw the pain flash across his eyes when she called him Daven and was confused again. *Why did it hurt him when she called him by name?*

"I don't deserve you, Sherry," he said as he turned and walked away.

Sheridan sat back down and closed her eyes. Why was she so drawn to this man? Why did it hurt so much?

Chapter Six

Aleksei walked out of Sheridan's office and started down the street. He wasn't overly surprised to see Joe stepping out and joining him.

"Everything okay, Boss?" Joe asked.

Aleksei wasn't used to confiding in anyone. Even with Daven, he would keep things bottled up to protect his friend. For some reason it felt right to tell Joe his concerns. He respected Joe and didn't feel like he needed to protect him.

"I'm hurting her, Joe. I think I'm falling in love with her and I know she feels the same. Where is the heartmate bond? How can I be falling in love with someone who isn't my mate?" Aleksei asked, in agony over his dilemma.

"I think you need to trust your instincts. What does your wolf tell you?" Joe asked.

"It wants her but without the heartmate bond, there is no mating. I won't hurt her worse than I already have," Aleksei said, as they reached Daven's sports car and climbed in.

"Aleksei, I've known and been watching you for a while now and I know that I trust your instincts. Why can't you trust them?" Joe asked.

"That's a good question. I've always trusted my instincts before. Speaking of instincts, it occurred to me today that we are looking in the wrong place for our stranger. No one in Daven's company would want to get rid of him, and everything we have discovered so far supports that. If they did the company would fail, and any insider would be losing a lot of money. We should be looking for a competitor. Who would get those government contracts if Daven's company went under?" Aleksei asked, as they drove back to Daven's estate.

"Let's find out," Joe said, as he dialed Penny's number at Isanti, Inc.

§

Aleksei sighed as he walked back through Shadow to Daven's estate. Daven and Penny had been married in a beautiful ceremony the day before. They planned to honeymoon in Hawaii for a week and then come back to the estate to begin their lives together.

Aleksei opened drawers and picked out a few items. He needed to head home to New Mexico to finish up several other projects, but hesitated. More than anything, he wanted to go to Sheridan and tell her everything. If only the heartmate bond would snap into place. Sighing and shaking his head, he put the clothes in a leather sack to Shadow Walk back to his apartment at Isanti, Inc. He was receiving daily reports from Joe about Sheridan. That would have to do until the heartmate bond snapped into place proving she was his mate.

Watching Penny and Daven tie the knot yesterday had been bitter sweet. The whole tribe had come except those Shadow Walkers who were on duty. Aleksei celebrated with his friend but at the same time felt very alone. His mother figured out something bothered him but he didn't want to take the attention away from Daven and Penny. Besides what would he have said, *I'm falling in love with a woman and I don't know if she's my mate?* That would have upset the whole tribe.

When the wedding party dispersed and his family had Shadow Walked back to his parent's house, his father suggested a run in wolf form. Aleksei jumped at the chance glad for the distraction. They stripped and shifted, and then ran out the large dog door in the back of the house into the surrounding woods.

Aleksei let himself run his hardest, setting the pace. His father stayed with him. Anyone seeing them would have been surprised to see a black wolf and a silver grey wolf running flat out together. They were both bigger than American wolves and because of their size could appear quite fearsome. Which is why they ran in Glacier National Park and stayed away from places inhabited by men.

After several miles, Aleksei slowed down, breathing hard. They needed to get home sometime tonight. The moon reflected on the white snow, making it almost like daylight to Aleksei and Sergei's eyes. Aleksei started rolling himself in the powder, while his father snorted at him.

He wouldn't find the fresh smells and winter wonderland of home in Beverly Hills. His father came up and nudged him. It was time to go back but he dragged his feet anyway. His father would worry about his mate and being separated. Such was the way of the Shadow Walker Wolf Clan.

Aleksei suddenly wondered if becoming CEO of Isanti, Inc. was really what he should be doing. It would mean a lot of hard work, long hours, and meetings, always more meetings. Could he deal with all that and a mate? Was that what he really wanted or was that what he thought he wanted?

Aleksei followed close on his father's tail as they ran through the snow. His mind touched his father's telepathically.

What do you think about me becoming CEO of Isanti, Inc? he sent.

You must do what will make you happy. All we want for you is your happiness.

What if my happiness is nothing more than finding a mate and settling down? He sent to his father.

Then that is what you should do. Be true to your heart.

What about making money and having a profession? Aleksei sent.

With the money you already have made and your inheritance, why do you need to make more? A profession needs to be more than making money. A profession means embracing your work, being the best at it you can be, and at the end of the day, satisfied that you did your best on that day. There must be the satisfaction of doing it, in everything you do, or why do it? sent his father.

I do feel satisfaction in working for Isanti. I guess I'm afraid I would lose that satisfaction if I had someone waiting at home for me. I'm afraid I would rather be at home with my mate than at work.

We, who share a wolf spirit, have that problem, needing to be with our mate all the time. It is the pack mentality to hunt with her, play with her, to love her, and raise your pups with her. When you are separated from your pack you feel lost and lonely. Already you struggle with loneliness, am I right? It is wise to think on these matters. You and your mate's happiness is all that really matters, his father explained to him.

Aleksei didn't know what the answer was yet but knew he had no choice but to be true to his wolf and himself.

Early the next morning, Aleksei Shadow Walked into the control room in Daven's house, with his satchel over his shoulder. He wanted to check the tapes for the past couple of days. He didn't really expect to see anything but it was the right thing to do.

He had gone more than halfway through the footage when the cameras on the motion sensors started picking something up. He couldn't believe it when he saw a man dressed in black climb down the mountain behind the house and cut a hole in the chain link fence with wire cutters. Aleksei looked at the time stamp on the camera and realized that it happened at three AM this morning.

"Shit, he could still be here," Aleksei said, as he dropped his stuff, stripped, and shifted to wolf.

He sniffed the air but didn't smell anything, and then started to make a search of the house. If the intruder had gotten in the house why hadn't the alarms gone off? Isanti's security team should have been notified electronically and someone would have let him know even during a wedding. Aleksei sent a mental call to Joe.

The perimeter was breached at Daven's estate at three AM this morning. I am on site, need back up.

Roger. Do not leave the house until I am on site. I'll bring a team with me in three.

Aleksei knew for Joe to be here in three minutes meant he hustled. Aleksei had reached the top of the stairs and looked down into a disaster. The house had definitely been breached. In fact, the front door stood open.

Aleksei saw the mess but was still cautious as he came downstairs. He could smell his intruder now but the scent was old. He was pretty sure the guy was gone. Aleksei moved from room to room. Each one had been trashed. Furniture was broken and ripped. The intruder had even spray painted on the walls. He had left a message behind, in big red letters across the living room wall. "You will die."

Aleksei realized as he looked at the wall that whoever the intruder was he wasn't sane. This wasn't about business or contracts. This was personal. Aleksei finished his search of the house but the intruder was long gone.

He stepped out on the front porch to find Sheridan getting out of her car. Aleksei figured the intruder must have gone out the open front gate. It was too late to shift. He stood on the landing baring the entrance and watched to see what her reaction would be to his wolf.

Sheridan looked at him in amazement.

"Wow. Well aren't you a handsome fellow," she said, moving toward him and holding out her hand.

Aleksei sniffed at her hand like a dog would and then gave her a big lick as he wagged his tail. Sheridan buried her hands in his fur and scratched behind his ears. Aleksei whined and nudged her. Sheridan dutifully continued to pet him and rub his ears. She seemed to have no fear of him. He felt warmth in his chest, glad that she could accept his wolf. Of course, right now, she thought he was a big dog. What would she think if she knew he was a man?

"You're such a big boy, a small child could ride on your back. Now where is your master? Doesn't he know not to leave his gate open, or the front door either? Of course, you would probably take care of the bad guys, wouldn't you handsome?" Sheridan crooned to him.

Then Joe came running out the front door.

"Alek, didn't I tell you to wait for me...." he said, before he saw Sheridan standing there.

"Is that his name? Alek? He's beautiful, what breed is he?" Sheridan asked, her hands still buried in Aleksei's ruff.

"Miss Harbrook, I didn't know you were here. We've had a break in and I'm afraid the police are on the way."

"Oh, no." She turned to the gate. "That must be why the gate was open." Just as quickly, she turned back to Joe. "Is Daven okay? He wasn't home, was he? He said he had a wedding yesterday," Sheridan went on.

"No, he wasn't home, but I must ask you to leave. The police will be here in a few minutes. I don't think you should be here when they arrive," Joe said, walking up and grabbing her arm. Joe herded her to the car but she still had her fingers wrapped in Aleksei's hair and he was forced to follow her.

"Please, Miss Harbrook," Joe said, letting some of the exasperation he felt into his voice.

"Okay, Joe. I'm going," she said.

Then she leaned down and hugged Aleksei's neck. He gave her a big lick on the face and wagged his tail at her, before she let go.

"See you later, Alek. Be a good dog." She got into her car and rolled down the window. "Please have Daven call me, Joe. The decorations are in and we need to get them up."

"I will, miss. Please drive carefully," Joe said, as he watched her turn around and drive away.

Aleksei went back into the house and up to the master bedroom where he shifted back into human form. He finishing fastening the buttons on his shirt, when Joe walked in.

"She's right, you are a handsome dog."

Aleksei showed his teeth and growled. "That's handsome wolf, to you."

"Okay, Boss, just teasing," Joe said, holding his hands up. "Ben is in the control booth. Brad and two others are on the perimeter. Looks like the intruder cut the power to the front gate to get it to open. He smashed the keypad next to the pool house to get in the house. I'm not sure why the alarms didn't go off. Ben will let us know if we have a picture of the intruder's face. I don't know why he didn't come upstairs, maybe somebody scared him away."

"I don't think anyone scared him. He left his message and then, he was done," Aleksei said, quietly. "Don't touch anything downstairs, we'll want pictures of everything, just like it is. I hope Daven has good insurance, this could cost him."

"Penny will love the fact that she has to redecorate. I've personally helped her paint her apartment three times. My sister's always moving furniture and buying knick-knacks," Joe said.

"Well, this will be right up her alley then," Aleksei said. "I want twenty-four-hour security on this place. One man on each side of the perimeter, and one man in the control room. I want to know why the alarms didn't go off at Isanti. If they did go off, why the hell no one moved on it. This is your department, Joe, find the problem and fix it!" Aleksei Shadow Walked into his office at Isanti, Inc.

§

Joe knew he deserved that last remark. He also knew Aleksei was mad as hell. Joe was almost glad Aleksei had left. It would give him the time to find the answers he needed for both their sakes. Someone in Isanti security had screwed up, and badly. Joe, as head of security, would find out who it was and bust them. He doubted the person would still have a job at Isanti, but it wouldn't be a part of his security department. The whole company had a reputation for being the best at what they did. Failures like this were not acceptable.

Joe pulled out his cell phone and called the Isanti security duty supervisor.

"I want to know who was on the alarms last night."

Joe couldn't believe what he heard. The person scheduled had called in sick. Because of the wedding there wasn't anyone to get the call. The person on the shift before had thought her replacement ran late. So, she had left and gone to the wedding reception.

Joe wanted to shout in frustration, evidently his department needed to be tightened up. There had been a complete breakdown in operations. No one should have left the control room unattended, even if there was a wedding to go to. He grabbed the laptop in the control room and sat down to write some new policies. Then he wrote his letter of resignation. This was his department and his failure. First, he had police showing up downstairs and a meeting of all the security department staff to set. He'd fix this mess before he tendered his resignation.

§

Sheridan hummed along with the Christmas Carols on the radio. She really liked Daven's new dog, Alek. She couldn't get over how big and beautiful he was. His eyes had seemed so intelligent and his black fur had felt so silky in her fingers. She couldn't resist loving on him. She had always been fond of animals but had given them up when her mother became ill. She had really wanted to stay and pet Alek and even thought about asking Joe to let him come visit with her for a while. Which was ridiculous, because she needed to go to work and where would she put a dog. But touching him had seemed to calm her in a way she'd never experienced before.

Sheridan didn't really know why she had driven out to Daven's house today. She could have just called but she missed him. She had hoped to at least see him even though he might not be back from the wedding. It was a silly thing to do, but she felt almost called to go.

She worried when she saw the front gate open but thought maybe they were receiving a delivery. Then she became concerned when she pulled up to the front of the house and saw the front door standing open. Then the big black dog walked out and nothing else seemed to matter but touching him. She could have petted him and rubbed his ears all day.

Sheridan smiled and then gave herself a little shake. *Wake up to reality and get back to work.* Daven McCloud's wasn't the only Christmas Party she was coordinating this month. She had four others before Daven's party and a New Year's Eve party as well. Her office was busy, busy, and she needed to stop thinking about a dog. In fact, she still needed a color scheme for the New Year's celebration. She could just picture Alek the dog in a purple and silver party hat. *That's it. Purple and silver with touches of black would be perfect for a New Year's Extravaganza.* Sheridan hoped her clients thought so as well.

She went back to singing Christmas Carols along with the radio.

Caryn Moya Block

Chapter Seven

Another week passed before Sheridan found her way back to Daven's estate. The outside decorations were loaded in every available space in the company van. Joe called, saying she could begin decorating today, but only outside. *Why only outside?* Time to get the decorations up was at a premium. It also hurt that Joe had called and not Daven.

Sheridan pulled up to the gate. An armed guard checked her identification before waving her through. That was unsettling, seeing the very visible increase in security, in addition to the gate. She pulled up to the front door and started unloading the van when Alek, the dog, came and stuck his nose in her crotch. Sheridan laughed and knelt down to hug the dog around the neck.

"I missed you too, handsome. Where's your master, huh? Did you give him the slip? Oh look, you have a nice new shiny name tag on your collar. That neon orange looks good against your black fur. Yes, it does," she said, rubbing his ears.

"Can I give you a hand, Miss Harbrook?" Joe asked, coming up to the car.

"Hi, Joe. Please call me Sheridan, especially if we keep meeting like this. Can you carry those tree shaped topiaries to the landing and then the big round ball topiaries go out by the pool. Don't worry, I'll place them when I get there," she answered.

Sheridan pulled out wreaths for the doors and upper front windows when she realized Alek, the dog, had disappeared. She tried not to feel disappointed. It would be easier to work without a dog underfoot.

She had stacked all the wreaths and tried to juggle them as she walked when she bumped into someone and started to fall. Strong hands grabbed her waist and held on to steady her. Sheridan's face reddened when she realized that one of the hands held bare flesh. An electrical charge zapped through her. She had worn jeans and a t-shirt to work today so she could climb ladders and wrestle lights onto bushes. The shirt, though one of her favorites, had shrunk up enough to just cover her stomach. It probably moved up as she balanced the wreaths.

"I'm so sorry, I didn't see you. Thank you for catching me. If you could let go now...." Sheridan paused as she felt the hand on her flesh caress her lightly. Then the hands were taking half of the wreaths off her stack and she could see the person in front of her.

"Hi," she said, all breathy. She cleared her throat. "I hoped you were here," Sheridan admitted, as she felt her heart thump wildly and her body tremble.

Daven smiled at her, that killer smile that made her breath catch. He wore jeans like her and a cobalt polo shirt that brought out the color of his eyes. On his feet were navy canvas boat shoes.

"Why, so you had someone to run into?" he teased

"So, I had someone to catch me when I did."

Daven turned and put the wreaths on the landing then took her stack and put them with the others. He reached out really slowly and pulled her into his arms.

"I'll always catch you when you fall, Sherry," he whispered, before he kissed her.

Sheridan felt the difference in this kiss immediately. Where before his kisses had been soft and gentle, this kiss, hard and demanding, was almost a claiming. It took her breath away. She felt Daven stiffen, and then Joe walked around the side of the house. She tried to pull away and put some distance between them but Daven wouldn't allow it. He held her firmly but gently.

"Sorry to interrupt, Boss. You have a call. It's Penny and her husband," Joe said.

Daven released her and stepped back, his face looking concerned.

Who is Penny? Sheridan wondered.

"I'll be back, Sherry," he murmured to her, before turning and walking inside the house.

Sheridan watched him. There was a fine behind on Daven McCloud. She could watch that man walk away from her and still enjoy the view. She glanced up and saw that Joe noticed her interest in Daven.

"Like what you see?" he teased her.

"More than is good for me, I'm afraid," Sheridan admitted.

"Be patient, he'll fall in line. Just give him a little more time," Joe said.

"You think so?" Sheridan asked, hope blooming in her chest.

"Oh, yeah. I know so," Joe said, smiling.

Joe and Sheridan finished unloading her car. Then Sheridan got to work.

§

Why is it every time I finally have Sheridan in my arms, someone interrupts us? Aleksei asked himself as he went inside. He picked up the phone.

"Daven?" Aleksei asked.

"Hey, bra. How's it?" Aleksei heard Daven say.

"Sounds like you're having fun in Hawaii. How's Penny?"

"My lovely wife is here beside me and it's *had* fun in Hawaii. We're on our way home," Daven said.

"Well good for you. Are Penny's parents glad you're back?"

"Not home to Montana, Alek. Home here, Beverly Hills."

"Didn't you get my messages? Didn't you see what this guy did to your house and wants to do to you? Why are you coming here?" Aleksei asked, angry with his friend for endangering himself and Penny.

"I can't keep running away, Alek. It's my home, no, our home now. We want to make it a home, together. In spite of the risks. I'll see you in a few minutes. You can yell at me then," Daven said, and then hung up. *Daven hung up on him?*

Aleksei couldn't believe Daven would just show up. What was he supposed to do with Sheridan being here? He had been fighting everything, including his own instincts, to keep this secret. Now the ruse would be blown to hell.

Aleksei paused, and then smiled. *He had been fighting his instincts, but why? Sheridan would understand his need to protect his friend. If he couldn't trust his instincts, what could he trust?*

He had wanted to tell her the truth since the beginning. Now, he really had no choice. Aleksei went to find Sheridan. He just hoped she wouldn't be too mad or disappointed with his deception.

Sheridan was in the back by the pool house setting up two large ball shaped topiaries along the center of the pool, one on each side. She told Joe to find an extension cord or two as Aleksei arrived. He nodded at Joe and sent a mind touch.

Daven and Penny will be arriving shortly. Make sure the perimeter is secure. Get them in the house as quickly as possible. I don't want anyone being able to get a shot at them.

Roger, Boss. What about your mate? Joe sent.

That's why I'm here.

Good luck, Aleksei

Thanks, I may need it.

Aleksei walked up and put his arms around Sheridan's waist. She reached high, placing the ball on top of the urn. She turned around in his arms and rested her hands on his shoulders.

"Hey, where have you been?" she chided him.

Aleksei wanted nothing more than to kiss Sheridan senseless. He didn't have a lot of time to get this explanation out. He kissed her on the nose.

"Can I talk to you a minute?" Aleksei asked as he took her by the hand and led her into the pool house.

"Is something the matter?"

"You mean besides the fact that I want you so badly I can barely stop myself from pushing you down on a chaise and having my way with you?" Aleksei asked.

Sheridan laughed. Aleksei prayed she would still be willing to laugh with him when he finished.

"Just tell me, Daven. I saw that flinch," Sheridan said.

"I'm not Daven McCloud. My name is Aleksei Sokolov. Daven is my best friend," Aleksei started.

"Aleksei?" Sheridan asked.

"I'm sorry I lied to you but someone is trying to kill Daven. I've assumed Daven's identity to protect him," Aleksei explained.

"Well, that explains the increase in security and the armed guards. Is that why you said it wasn't safe around you and it wasn't safe for you to admit how you felt?" Sheridan asked, quietly. "Is that why you cringed each time I called you Daven? I couldn't figure out how my saying your name was so painful to you."

"It was painful. I wanted so badly for you to know me, Aleksei, not me as Daven. Please forgive me, Sherry. I didn't do it to hurt you. I told you the truth when I said I would never hurt you on purpose."

"Why now? What changed your mind?" Sheridan asked.

Aleksei knew from her tone she expected him to say something romantic, like "I couldn't take it anymore and had to have you." Or "My love for you was so strong I could no longer deny it." But that wouldn't be honest. Sheridan deserved the truth.

"I won't deny that I'm glad you now know the situation. I hated the fact that you thought I was Daven and wanted to correct you more than once. The reason I changed my mind is Daven and his new bride, Penny, will be arriving shortly. I didn't want you hurt when you saw them together."

"Why do you think I would be hurt?" Sheridan asked, in a puzzled tone of voice.

"I worried that if you saw Daven, with Penny on his arm, and thought it was me, it would hurt you."

"I suppose if I saw Daven, and thought it was you, it would hurt. Why do you think I wouldn't be able to tell the two of you apart?" she asked.

"Sheridan, Daven and I are like twins. That's why I was here to begin with."

Sheridan shook her head and sighed. "Thank you for finally telling me the truth. What does hurt is that you didn't feel you could trust me. I understand you trying to protect your friend." Her eyes narrowed slightly. "Tell me, Aleksei, who protects you?"

She turned and walked out of the pool house. Anger radiated off her like a propane heater in winter. Sheridan started towards the front of the house and her van. Aleksei followed like a hurt puppy.

"Sherry?" he asked, quietly.

Waving him off, she responded, "It's okay, Aleksei. I just need to get away for a while. I'll be back tomorrow to finish up the outside decorations. I need to buy more extension cords anyway."

"I don't want to lose you, Sherry," Aleksei said.

Sheridan spun so quickly he almost didn't see it. She started poking him in the chest, her body quivering with emotion.

"I don't want to lose you either, you idiot. You didn't think of *that* when you were here every day making a target of yourself, did you. Why don't you hang a sign? 'Kill Me' around your neck! Did you think it would impress me? Because it doesn't, it terrifies me." Sheridan burst into tears.

Aleksei pulled her close letting her cry it out. He was happy to see she had such strong feelings for him. She certainly wasn't afraid to show them.

"Let me take you inside and we'll talk about this some more," Aleksei said.

"No, I want to go home. Remember one thing, Aleksei Sokolov. I'll be miserable without you so don't you dare get hurt."

§

Sheridan pulled away from him and headed around the front of the house rubbing the tears from her eyes. She wasn't overly surprised when Joe stepped up and led her to the passenger side of her car, taking the keys away from her.

"Let me guess, he wants you to drive me home," Sheridan said.

"As miserable as you would be without him, he would be worse without you. In fact, he might not recover if something happened to you. He just wants to ensure your safety."

They got into the car, buckled up, and Joe started the engine.

"Don't be overly dramatic, Joe."

"I'm not, Sheridan. Lycans cannot live without their mates," Joe said, as he turned the car around and headed back out to the street.

"Lycan? What's that?" she asked.

Joe told her. About the Lycans, the heartmate bond, and about Aleksei's wolf spirit.

"I don't believe it. A wolf?"

"It's true. I wouldn't lie to you, I never have," Joe insisted.

"You're not playing some kind of elaborate joke, are you?"

"I think you know me well enough to answer that question on your own."

"Wait, Alek...Aleksei. Alek the dog ... was Aleksei?"

"Yeah. He got a little testy when he found the name tag I added to that silly orange collar." Joe chuckled.

"What's silly is I think I'm falling for him, Joe. Tell me everything about these Lycans."

§

Daven and Penny are secure in the house, came the telepathic report. Aleksei found his friends in the library. Penny had her tablet, while Daven measured the space under the window. When Penny saw him enter, she squealed and grabbed him for a hug. Daven walked up and hugged him as well. They both looked happy and content. Aleksei had missed both of them.

"Welcome home," Aleksei said.

"What, no lecture on how it's not safe to be here?" Daven asked, teasing his friend.

"Would it change your mind?" Aleksei asked.

"No, and you already know that don't you," Daven said.

Daven didn't like the shadows in his friend's eyes. Other than that, Aleksei seemed even more self-assured than before the wedding. It used to irritate him at how calm and grounded Aleksei could be. Now, Daven had Penny. Her love and acceptance grounded him like nothing else could. It was something that he never expected to happen. He also began to listen to his inner voice. Because Penny had faith in him and wanted his happiness, Daven found himself being true to his nature and not playing the games learned from his parents. Penny was his soul mate. He had slowly realized how far away from his own desires he had drifted. All that really mattered to him now was making a future together with his wife.

The first step was to take his life back and stop whoever tried to scare him and threatened to kill him. This was his home, and no one would chase him away. Aleksei didn't argue or try to talk them out of it. He listened and let them tell him their plan. It was a little risky but he and Penny both thought it would work.

"You are going to make it tough to keep you safe, Daven. You're baiting the killer."

"We'll have a whole crew at the party watching everyone," Penny said.

"I'll be careful. Believe me, I've everything to live for now that I have Penny," Daven said, turning to his wife.

"You're such a sweet talker," Penny said, patting his cheek.

Penny picked up the phone to call a painting crew to come out to the house tomorrow. Daven, with Aleksei's help, took measurements of the now empty rooms.

The Library was the only room that was still in good condition. The intruder had dumped out the books and knocked out the shelves of the bookcases. It had been an easy fix to pick up the books and rearrange the shelves. The room only needed a couple of chairs and reading lamps to be ready for the party.

The front room and dining room sustained the most damage. The intruder had destroyed everything in those two rooms. When the clean-up crew removed the ruined carpet, they found beautiful hardwood floors underneath. In the kitchen, the dishes had been pulled from the cabinets and smashed.

Aleksei purchased a set of Majorcan Pottery as a wedding gift for Penny and Daven and replaced the counter stools so he had a place to eat. Penny would pick out a new table set later.

"You've really cleaned everything up," Daven said to Aleksei. "When you sent the pictures of the damage, I didn't think we could get so far so quickly. I can't thank you enough for taking care of things."

"That's what friends are for, right?" Aleksei asked.

For Daven's plan to work, the house needed to be ready to entertain and the new household staff needed to be hired and in place. Penny was ultimately in charge of both the decorating and interviewing of staff. Everyone else would pitch in when asked and make sure nobody sneaked in again. They had twelve days to get ready for the party and set the trap for their intruder.

The house was protected. All power sources were hidden and the destroyed keypads had been replaced. Battery backups were installed in case of a power outage, as well as a generator, for longer outages. The crew had also integrated new smoke and carbon dioxide alarms into the system. A fire sprinkler system had been installed in the garage. With the guards in place, Daven's house was as secure as Aleksei could make it.

§

Joe didn't feel bad about telling Sheridan about Aleksei, though he cautioned her not to let anyone know, ever. He owed his Boss and if he could help him with this, so be it.

Aleksei denied his letter of resignation and implemented all the policy and operational changes Joe had suggested. Then stood with him, as Joe dressed down his personnel and explained the changes were effective immediately. Aleksei turned on the computer and showed them a video of what had been done to Daven's house. Then he asked them one question in a quiet voice.

"What would have happened if Daven and Penny had been home that night?"

Everyone got the message really quickly. Joe was impressed again with Aleksei Sokolov and his leadership. He didn't yell, or rant. He explained what had happened and the impact. He had a professional team and he expected nothing less than their best efforts.

It was a proud team, and they each took a sense of personal responsibility for the breakdown. If one of them failed, then they all failed their client, Joe, Aleksei, Isanti, and themselves. It would not happen again.

Alek wasn't finished. He expected everyone to spend half a work day cleaning up the mess inside the house.

Aleksei hadn't asked for more, but many people stayed longer. He'd suggested that since they had not observed or prevented the break-in from happening, the least they could do was help clean it up. So, when Daven and Penny walked into the house, they would find the place spotless. Even the spray paint had been cleaned off. A lot of the rooms were empty but anything salvageable they fixed.

It made people feel better to be helping and a fund had been generated to pay for new furniture. Another reason Joe liked Aleksei's leadership. He corrected the situation and made people feel glad they contributed. There were no hard feelings or bad tempers.

When Joe told Sheridan what Aleksei had accomplished. She'd started crying again. Joe stopped at a gas station for a box of Kleenex.

Arriving at her home Joe walked Sheridan to her door. She thanked him with a kiss on the cheek.

"Take care of him for me," she said.

"Don't worry. It will be my pleasure," Joe said.

He didn't want Aleksei to smell Sheridan on him, so once Sheridan had locked her front door, he Shadow Walked to the gas station to wash the kiss off. Then he Shadow Walked back to Daven's house. He found everyone in the front room when he materialized in the foyer.

"I told Sheridan the truth. She knows our secrets now..."

"You did what?" Aleksei growled.

§

Later that evening, Aleksei picked up the phone to call Sheridan. He had hurt her and was missing her. He needed to know if she was okay after what Joe told her. *Why didn't the heartmate bond snap into place?*

Caryn Moya Block

Chapter Eight

The next day dawned brightly and Sheridan was once again on her way to Daven McCloud's estate, but completing the party decorations weren't the only things racing through her mind. She slept little and was excited to see Aleksei and learn more about his Lycan tendencies.

She drove up to the front gate and waited as the guard checked her ID and waved her through, like yesterday. Driving up to the house, she examined the row of topiaries lining the drive that had been set yesterday. When the lights were on it would look very festive.

Today, she needed to hang the wreaths on the upstairs windows and connect all the light cords into a timer system. She had gone out and purchased more extension cords and now felt confidant everything would be finished outside today.

The inside decorations had yet to begin and Sheridan wanted to talk to someone about it. The fresh greenery had arrived and needed to be put up. It would be dropping needles soon anyway but if they left it in plastic too long it would start to rot.

Then there was the question of whom she should speak to about these things. Daven was the name on the contract but Aleksei had signed it. She wasn't really concerned, but it wasn't legal and new paperwork needed to be created. Maybe, Sheridan could talk to Daven's wife.

She pulled up to the front door and parked the car. The front drive was crowded with a couple vans with a painting company logo. As if on cue, part of a painting crew appeared, coming and going through the entrance. Sheridan wondered where she might find Aleksei as she opened the trunk. She shook her head when she noticed the mess from the bags shifting. Hopefully, Aleksei would find her. She smiled. She was certain of it.

Sheridan put her head in the trunk, gathering the electrical cords into a bag. Suddenly, arms snaked around her waist. How many times had Aleksei snuck up and put his arms around her? *This wasn't Aleksei.* Sheridan was furious.

"I suggest you unhand me this minute," she said, turning around and finding herself in someone's arms. Someone who looked like Aleksei but wasn't.

"Come on, Baby, it's me," Daven said, nuzzling her. Sheridan started pushing against him and struggling.

"Let go of me this instant Daven. How dare you try your silly games with me!" She yelled as she pushed him.

§

The gate guard informed Aleksei that Sheridan had arrived and he started for the front door when Penny stopped him to ask his opinion on the new paint color.

A tingle of pure energy shot through him. He didn't know why, but Sheridan was furious. He ran out the door before Penny could stop him.

He stepped outside to see Sheridan struggling in Daven's arms. Rage as he had never known rushed through Aleksei. He wanted to kill Daven for touching her. He ran down the stairs. Joe appeared suddenly and grabbed his arm, holding him. Aleksei growled.

He looked toward Sheridan. She punched Daven in the face and he fell to the ground. Joe let go and a racing Aleksei caught Sheridan in his arms. He shook with rage but held her gently to him.

"Are you all right, Sherry? Are you hurt?" he asked her softly.

She wrapped her arms around his waist and held on tight. Joe stood quietly, watching. Daven wisely stayed on the ground.

"No, but I hope he is. I'm sorry, Aleksei. Daven McCloud is an Ass," she said and then snuggled closer.

Aleksei felt calm sink into him. It was almost like Sheridan used some kind of psychic ability to calm his rage. He turned and looked at his friend. Daven's nose looked broken. Aleksei didn't feel a hint of concern even seeing the blood running down Daven's face.

Penny stood on the top of the steps, having followed Aleksei to the door. Her eyes wide with fear and worry. She had seen Aleksei almost go for Daven.

"Daven, I could have killed you. If Joe hadn't stopped me, I would have. Don't *ever* touch Sheridan again. If you do, I won't be held responsible," Aleksei said.

Then he led Sheridan around the house to the pool room. He stood for a moment and just held her. It surprised him that he had gotten so angry. If he didn't know better, he'd think he was in the throes of the mating heat. But there was no cord tying their hearts together. Aleksei looked down at Sheridan. She watched him waiting.

"Your eyes are still flashing golden," she whispered to him.

"It's my wolf spirit. He wanted to tear out Daven's throat for daring to touch you. Now he wants me to claim you as my mate."

"What does the claiming entail? You didn't describe that when we talked on the phone."

"You mean besides a tribal ceremony?"

"I guess so, what else?"

"Well, it's kind of awkward talking about claiming over the phone. Claiming means, I take you to bed and we stay there for a couple of weeks while I learn every inch of your body and you learn mine."

"We can't do that?" Sheridan asked, after hearing the regret in Aleksei's voice.

"No, we can't. But someday, Sheridan, we will."

"Well, I'll have to check my calendar, but I'll try to keep it open for you," she teased him.

Aleksei laughed. Sheridan could do that, say the right thing to break a mood or surprise him and make him laugh. It was one of the many things he loved about her.

"Come on handsome. We've got work to do," she said, leading him back around the house.

§

Joe had felt Aleksei's rage rush through the tribal link and sensed it had something to do with Sheridan's arrival and immediately moved to the front of the mansion. He needed to get to Aleksei or someone would die. Joe saw the problem in a instant. His sister's new husband was an idiot, but he had to stop Aleksei from killing his best friend.

Joe might be risking his own life by trying to stop him. Aleksei's eyes were completely golden with the wolf. He bared his teeth and growled.

Luckily, Aleksei was still present enough to stop if only for a moment. Joe heard the sound of Daven's nose breaking and figured whatever happened, the guy deserved it. He had stood ready to stop Aleksei if he went for Daven again. Instead, Aleksei went to Sheridan and she calmed him. Joe felt the calm flow through the tribal link and a tiny wisp spread to the whole tribe. He watched as Aleksei led Sheridan away and then turned to his sister.

"You better attend to your mate," he said.

She rushed forward, telepathically calling Ben to get towels and ice as she cradled Daven's head in her lap.

"Oh, Daven," Penny said, with a sigh. "I told you testing Sheridan was a stupid idea."

Joe squatted down next to Daven. "For a man who just went through the mating process, you aren't too bright," Joe said, shaking his head.

"I didn't know he would get so mad. I was testing her, like we used to do in college," Daven said.

"Did she pass the test?" Joe asked, out of curiosity.

"With flying colors. The moment I touched her, she knew I wasn't Aleksei. What's going on between them? Penny said the heartmate bond didn't attach," Daven asked.

"I'm not sure but she's his mate. I'd bet my life on it." Joe said, smiling.

"You almost did. Thanks for stopping him," Daven said.

"I couldn't let him kill my new brother-in-law. For someone who claims to be Aleksei's best friend you don't know him that well. Don't ever get between a wolf and its mate, unless you're suicidal," Joe scolded.

"You're right, I don't know him as well as I should. How do I make this up to him?" Daven asked.

"The best thing to do is apologize and take responsibility for your actions. He'll respect you more that way. You might want to study up on wolf behavior. Aleksei may seem like the calmest person in the room but never forget a wolf lives in his soul."

Ben arrived with ice and towels and he and Joe helped Daven get up and walk into the house. Penny would Shadow Walk him to the infirmary in New Mexico. Joe suggested they stay in her apartment tonight at Isanti. When they got back tomorrow, Aleksei would be ready to hear Daven's apology. Joe wasn't sure if Aleksei would be ready before that.

He walked back outside in time to hear Aleksei laugh. Joe smiled to himself. Sheridan was just what Aleksei needed in a mate. She was fun and loving but also had a fiery temper and a great right cross. She also seemed to be an empath of some sort. Joe knew she must be pretty powerful to have sent that calm to the whole tribe. He wondered what else she could do.

§

Aleksei helped Sheridan finish the outside decorations. Then she coaxed him to shift into wolf form. Since the painters had left and only Isanti employees were on the grounds, he obliged her. They ran and played in the yard. First Sheridan chased Aleksei and then Aleksei chased Sheridan. He was careful not to be too rough with her but he loved to knock her down and then stand over her, licking her face until she begged him to stop. When she caught him, which was less frequent, she would lay on him and rub his tummy or ears. Aleksei was tempted to shift and let her rub his tummy as a human but knew that Joe and the guards were watching.

He saw Joe laughing as they raced around the trees in the yard. Finally, Sheridan sat down in the grass. Aleksei walked up and plopped down next to her, his head in her lap.

"I had a lot of fun today," she said, as she petted his head. "I'm sorry about what happened with Daven. I never meant to come between you."

Aleksei nudged at her thigh with his nose.

"I know you don't blame me. After all you've done for him, well, you must love him. I'm just saying don't be too hard on him. In his own way, he was trying to protect you. He may be an Ass but he's still your best friend," Sheridan said, hugging Aleksei around his neck.

Sheridan pushed him gently off her lap.

"I've got to go, I have a party tonight. Call me when you can. The greenery is in and I need to get it installed before it gets all yucky."

She stood and brushed herself off. Aleksei leaped up and put his paws on her shoulders, then he licked her nose. Sheridan laughed and hugged him.

"I love you too, Aleksei. I'll see you soon. Don't worry about shifting, just get up on the stairs, so I know you're not going to be hit by the car."

Her concern warmed his heart and he obediently went up the steps. Sheridan climbed into her car, turned it around, and waving out the window drove away.

When would the mating bond show itself?

Aleksei felt happier than he ever had before and had Sheridan to thank for it. He jumped off the stoop and ran as fast as he could around the perimeter. Then he bounded back up the steps and let out a howl of celebration. Sheridan accepted him as wolf and as a man. When the time was right, she would accept him as mate.

§

Sheridan watched Aleksei in his wolf form as she drove away. He was such a good-looking wolf. She loved running her fingers through his hair and she had loved playing with him today. It had felt good to run around and stretch her muscles. Before her mother became ill, she had run every morning for exercise. She loved the feeling her body gave her of being in complete harmony of motion. Maybe they could run together, if Aleksei stuck around that is.

Sheridan knew he worked in New Mexico for Isanti, Inc. She also knew he was being groomed to take over as CEO. Could she compete with that? *Did she want to? And what about Enchanted Evenings?*

She told Aleksei she loved him today or rather she had told his wolf. It was true. She loved him, whether he was a man or a wolf. *Welcome to my crazy life...*

§

It was past midnight when Sheridan arrived home from her latest party success. She dragged off her clothes and laid on the bed. She should be exhausted and felt weary but all evening, she couldn't stop thinking of Aleksei, both man and wolf.

She jumped when her cell phone rang. Grabbing it, she quickly answered.

"Aleksei?"

"Sherry, I didn't expect you to answer. Is everything okay?" Aleksei asked.

"Yes, I got in a little while ago. I was thinking about you," Sheridan dared to say.

"I think about you too, *milaya*."

"What does that mean?" Sheridan asked.

"It's Russian, and means 'sweet or dearest'. My dad often calls my Mom by the endearment. I hope you don't mind."

"No, it's *sweet*," Sheridan said, chuckling.

Aleksei laughed. "Maybe that's why we make such a great pair. We're both sweet but after that punch you hit Daven with, I'd say you are a might spicy too."

"Spicy, huh?"

"In a totally good way," Aleksei quickly added. "I called to let you know that the house should be ready for decorating tomorrow afternoon. Maybe after you finish, we could get dinner."

"I'd like that..."

"Then, it's a date. Sleep well. I'll see you tomorrow."

"Good night," Sheridan said. She lay on the bed and stared at the ceiling with a big smile on her face.

§

The next afternoon, Sheridan pulled up to Daven's estate. Hopefully, Aleksei was here. She couldn't stop thinking of his smile. A thrill of excitement rushed up her spine every time she saw him. Now if only they could have some time together alone.

She parked her car near the front and began to unload the garlands from her trunk. The delivery of trees, she had ordered, stood near the door. Finally, she could decorate inside. She grabbed her tool kit from the back seat.

Joe appeared as if by magic and began to carry things inside. Sheridan had him pick up the tree for the library and entered the foyer. Box upon box of decorations stood waiting to be unpacked. It would be a long day.

"What else can I do to help?" Joe asked.

Sheridan hesitated. She wanted to ask about Aleksei but her job here was to decorate for Christmas.

"Well, I could really use a ladder and if you happen to have some Christmas music we can put on that would be great. I like to decorate while listening to remind me of why I love Christmas."

Joe smiled. "I think I can arrange that for you. Aleksei isn't here at the moment but he should be arriving soon. I'll be right back." Joe headed deeper into the house.

Sheridan sighed and picked up the smallest tree before walking into the library. Daven's wife sat behind the desk using her laptop.

"Hi, I don't think we've been properly introduced. I'm Penny, Daven's wife."

"Hi," Sherry said, reminding herself that this was the real client, and she had punched her husband yesterday. "I'll try to stay out of your way."

"Don't worry about it. We're all so glad to have you. Aleksei loved the Christmas theme you two picked out. He told me all about it. I think it's going to look beautiful."

Suddenly, the sound of Bing Crosby singing about orange and palm trees swaying came over the speaker system.

"I hope you don't mind," Sheridan said, quickly.

"Not at all, I love Christmas music," Penny said. "We all need to get into the Christmas spirit around here."

Sheridan put the tree in the stand and then placed it in the corner as she and Aleksei had agreed. She stuck with the original plan discussed and hoped the real homeowners didn't object. Since Penny was busy on her computer, Sheridan decided to leave the library to decorate last. She went quietly into the living room. Glancing around the area which included the large foyer, Sheridan pictured the room already decorated. Joe had brought in a ladder for her and it leaned against the wall. Smiling, she reached for her tool kit and began the process of hanging the garlands near the ceiling.

§

Aleksei was late. He glanced at his watch, noting it was almost seven. Hopefully, Sheridan hadn't given up on him.

He walked down the staircase in Daven's home and gazed in wonder at the place. Between Penny's home furnishings and Sheridan's Christmas decorations, it looked like something out of a magazine. The gold and cream trimmings with a sprinkling of burgundy looked rich and exclusive, just the way he and Sheridan had envisioned.

He heard laughter in the library and followed the sound. Sheridan and Penny were laughing at Daven and the look on his face as he held up a cream ballerina ornament.

"If you really don't like it I can send it back," Sheridan said, chuckling.

"No," Penny said, quickly. "It's lovely. Daven is going to have to start letting some culture into his life."

"I let you in, didn't I?" Daven grumbled, but he laid the fragile ornament on the loveseat. "Oh, uh, Alek..." Daven said, seeing Aleksei in the doorway. "I owe you an apology about yesterday. I only wanted to make sure Sheridan was the right mate for you. She passed the test with an A+."

Aleksei waved at Daven but only had eyes for one person.

"Sheridan?"

He crossed the room to her. She looked lovely in a cream-colored blouse and black jeans. Her hair fell in russet curls around her shoulders.

"Hi," she said, her voice breathy. Aleksei drew her into his arms. Holding her filled him with the warmth he lost from walking through Shadow.

"I'm sorry, I'm late."

"It's okay," Sheridan said, color coming into her cheeks. "I'm actually not done with this last tree. Daven and Penny were helping me finish."

"Have you eaten? I can order something in. For all of us if you want," Aleksei said, turning to Penny and Daven.

"I'll get it," Daven said, jumping up. "It's the least I can do. I owe you, man."

"You just want to get out of helping to finish the tree," Penny said.

"You could come with me," Daven suggested, winking at her.

"You will come back with food, right?" Sheridan asked.

"Sure, sure..." Daven said.

"Don't worry. I'll make sure we get back right away. What do you feel like eating?" Penny asked.

"How about the best burgers there are, In and Out?" Daven asked.

"Anything works for me as long as it's quick," Sheridan said. "I'm starving."

"No worries," Daven said, taking Penny's hand and pulling her from the room.

Aleksei stood, holding Sheridan's hand as they heard the front door open and close.

"Alone at last," he said, pulling Sheridan back into his arms.

"I really need to finish this tree, Aleksei," she said, her voice barely above a whisper.

"I'll help you. After...this." He lowered his head to hers, watching her eyes for permission to kiss her.

She leaned forward and put her arms around his neck. He pressed his lips to hers and she sighed, opening for him. Their tongues tangled. A wave of desire filled him and he pulled her closer. Sheridan moaned and grabbed his head, holding him to her mouth. Aleksei growled low in his throat. *He wanted her. Now.*

A wave of warmth filled his chest and then.... He could feel Sheridan. Her passion flowed through him, doubling his own. Aleksei smiled and pulled back enough to glance down at his chest. A thin golden light glowed between them. *The heartmate bond! Finally.*

"Is something wrong?" Sheridan asked.

"No, everything is right."

Sheridan pulled farther away. "The tree. I really do need to finish it. Daven and Penny won't be that long."

She licked her lips. Aleksei felt his body respond but if his mate wanted to decorate a tree that is what they'd do.

§

Sheridan's body quivered with excitement. *Aleksei's kiss was ... Wow.* She smiled at him and walked over to the box of ornaments. It took all of her self-control to move away from him. She wanted to throw herself into his arms but instead reached into the box and took out another ornament. He wasn't her client anymore but she was still technically *working.*

"If you will unwrap the ornaments, I'll put them on the tree. We should be done by the time Daven and Penny get back with food."

"Anything you want, Sherry. We have all the time in the world."

Sheridan sighed as she chose a branch. "If only that were true. My mother is dying. She has Parkinson's disease. Slowly, each day, she gets worse. I've learned to cherish the moments I have but not to count on the future."

"I'm sorry about your mother. Is there anything I can do?"

"No." Sheridan shook her head. "When I came home from college to help, there were medicines that would treat the symptoms. Now it's hit or miss. They want me to put her in a home but I can't do it."

"You have help?" Aleksei began to unwrap the ornaments and put hooks on them.

"Yes, nurses come in and stay with her while I'm working. Luckily, Enchanted Evenings pays the bills." She placed the next ornament on the tree. "I don't know why I'm dumping this on you. Forgive me. I just wanted you to know." Sheridan took a deep breath. "Aleksei, I don't know how we could make it work with you in New Mexico and me here with my mother."

Aleksei nodded. "I wondered what was holding you back. After dinner, I'll show you how we can make this work."

§

No wonder the heartmate bond was only a thread in diameter. The situation with Sheridan's mother kept her from committing to him. He smiled and squinted his eyes, seeing the golden thread of light that ran from her heart to his. *She was his mate.* He would do whatever he could to help her.

He unwrapped another ornament and glanced in the box. There were only six ornaments left to hang. Sheridan walked over and picked up two more decorations and stepped back to study the tree.

"What are you looking for?" Aleksei asked.

"Empty spots, or places where the ornaments are too close together. A lot of people only put ornaments on the edge of the branches but I like to layer them back into the tree."

"Only a few left to go."

Aleksei put another hook on then reached for the last glass ball.

"Why don't you put one on? Of the three trees, I think I like this one best."

"You've done a beautiful job, Sherry. The house looks amazing."

Aleksei picked up the last two ornaments and walked over to the tree. He found the perfect spots and hung them on the branches.

"I need to take some pictures for my projects portfolio." Sheridan smiled. "Everything looks just like I imagined it."

"I'll hire a photographer. Consider it my Christmas present to you." Aleksei put his arm around her waist and pulled Sheridan into his side. They stood leaning into each other and gazing at the Christmas tree.

"I'm falling in love with you, Sherry, and you told my wolf you loved me, too." Aleksei turned and kissed her temple. "I know its soon but I want you to know I will do whatever is necessary to make this work."

"You will?" Sheridan asked, gazing up at him.

"Yes, *milaya*. I take everything you are into my keeping and give everything I am to you."

Sheridan rubbed at her chest and looked perplexed. "That sounds...interesting."

Aleksei laughed. "The words are a tradition of my people said from one mate to another."

"I feel different somehow. I think the words are more than a tradition."

"A vow then..."

"Food's here." Daven said, walking into the room. "You guys okay? We're setting the food out in the kitchen."

"Never better," Aleksei said, pulling Sheridan in for a kiss. Daven smartly withdrew back to the kitchen.

"Stay with me tonight. I'll pay for the nurses to stay overnight."

"I'll have to call and see," Sheridan said, her tone worried. "I guess we could go to my house..."

"Let me ask. If the nurse isn't willing to stay, we can schedule a night in the future. I don't want to pressure you if you're not ready, Sherry."

"It's not that. I've never had a man over to my parent's house. It's been a long time since I've had a man in my life, period."

"I'm not sorry to think you've been waiting for me, *milaya*. I promise to be gentle. We won't do anything you don't want to do."

"I know. I trust you, Alek."

"Hey guys, the burgers are getting cold," Daven called from the kitchen.

"We're coming," Aleksei answered.

§

Sheridan walked into her house alone. She bit her lip as she waved at the nurse. Then walking down the hall, she checked in on her mother. Quietly watching the rise and fall of her mother's chest, Sheridan wrapped her arms around her waist and squeezed. *Why does everything have to be so difficult?*

Sighing, she walked into her small room and began to disrobe. Leaving Aleksei tonight had been excruciatingly difficult. It was almost like a rubber band connected them and when she put distance between them, the band wanted to snap them back together. She could almost see it, a shimmering thread of light that connected them at the heart. If it wasn't for her mother, she would have stayed with Aleksei in a heartbeat.

She pulled down the covers and slipped into bed. Her eyes prickled with unshed tears. Hugging her pillow, she admitted she was tired but why did her heart feel like a piece was missing?

§

Aleksei slammed his hand down on his desk in New Mexico. More than anything he wanted to be back in California with his mate, but he'd gotten the call from Isanti, Inc. that the forensics department wanted to report their findings. *So much for some personal time with Sheridan.*

"What do you mean there are no leads? Didn't our facial recognition software come up with anything?"

"No. Whoever this guy is, we couldn't get a clear enough picture to get a match."

"He cut the chain link fence right in front of the cameras," Aleksei said, frustration making him want to shout.

"Yes, sir and he wore a ski mask to do it. I wish I could give you more. The fibers we found from the gloves he wore match a brand at a local convenience store. I've got a team searching the store's video footage located closest to the property but thousands of those gloves are sold this time of year. He could have purchased them anywhere nationwide."

"Okay," Aleksei said, sighing. He ran his hand through his hair. "Let me know if you figure anything out."

Aleksei put down the phone and stared out the window at the darkness. He'd hoped to at least get a clue about who their intruder might be. Daven's idea of setting himself up as bait could backfire with dire consequences. Aleksei didn't want to see his friend hurt or killed.

A quiver of awareness centered in his heart, causing it to ache. He put his hand to his chest. *What was that?*

The pain grew sharper. Aleksei closed his eyes and concentrated on what he felt. The pain came from the heartmate bond. *Sheridan?*

He reached for her with his telepathy following the thin thread of light that connected them at the heart. He could feel her. She sobbed.

What is it, Sherry? Why are you crying?

Aleksei? How can I hear you?

We are connected, love. I carry you with me in my heart. What has you so upset?

I'm sorry, I shouldn't be feeling sorry for myself. Sometimes I feel so alone.

Let me come to you. Open your eyes and look around the room. Is it dark?

Yes. I'm already in bed.

Pick the darkest corner and really stare at it. Send me the picture of what you are seeing.

Sheridan slowly built the picture in her mind until Aleksei could see it clearly. Turning off the light in his office, he kneeled down near the floor where the darkness wavered. Placing his hands palm to palm, he inserted them into the shadows and then pulled them apart to make a doorway. Still holding the picture of Sheridan's room in his mind, he stepped into the Shadow Dimension.

§

Sheridan sat up in bed and stared at the corner of the room. Something would happen, she felt it. Her eyes grew wide as the darkness got thicker and then Aleksei walked out of the shadows as if by magic.

"What was that?" she asked.

"That, *lyubov moya*, was Shadow Walking. I'll explain later." He sat on the edge of the bed and brushed his finger over her wet cheek. "You've been crying."

"I know. I'm not really sure why but I couldn't handle being away from you."

"The heartmate bond does that sometimes, makes us grieve when our mate is too far away. Scoot over, let me hold you." Aleksei climbed into the bed and pulled her next to him. She sighed and rubbed her face against his shoulder. She heard his shoes hit the floor.

"You were in Beverly Hills that's not far away." She looked up at him. His eyes seemed to be glowing with a golden sheen.

"I was in New Mexico, but I'm here now. Don't you want to know what the heartmate bond is?"

"I'm guessing it's that cord of light I see connecting us at the heart." Sheridan squinted her eyes and looked down at their chests.

"You can see it?" Aleksei asked, awe in his tone.

"Yes, and I can feel it pulling on me. Before you appeared, it felt like a rubber band strung too tight. It hurt."

"I'm sorry about that," Aleksei said, running his hand down her arm. "I didn't realize how sensitive you would be. Try something for me. Follow the cord of light into my heart. See if you can feel me."

Sheridan closed her eyes to concentrate. She pictured the golden thread of light and then somehow, she was in the light, flowing through to Aleksei. She could feel him. He surrounded her with love. Their minds, hearts, and souls merged. It was glorious. So much love... for her.

See? We are connected. All you have to do to find me, is reach through the heartmate bond. I am here with you. Nothing can part us, but death, and some say even that is temporary.

Wow. I'm amazed.

If you're amazed now. What do you think of this?

Chapter Nine

Aleksei leaned down and kissed her. Feathery kisses so gentle her eyes teared. Sheridan felt their combined pleasure from their merged senses. Desire spiked and she pressed her lips more firmly against his. He licked along the seam of her lips and she opened with a sigh. Threading her fingers through his hair, she pulled him closer.

I want you, she admitted.

I am yours.

Aleksei slipped open a button on her pajama top and then he touched her skin to skin. His warm hands felt wonderful as he caressed her breast and teased the tight nipple. A wave of desire had her skin sensitizing.

More, touch me more, she begged.

You're so beautiful.

She reached for the buttons on his shirt. He helped by shrugging the garment off. Then she pulled her own shirt off while Aleksei worked on his pants. In no time, there was only flesh.

Sheridan couldn't stop touching Aleksei. She had this crazy need to feel every inch of him. She loved how his chest hair tickled her skin. Burying her nose in his neck she licked over his pulse and then took in his smell of leather and musk.

Her hands drifted lower, lightly scoring his stomach and thigh before closing around his heavy erection. Aleksei growled and pushed against her hand. Every touch flowed through the heartmate bond. Every pleasure doubled and filled them both.

§

I will never get enough of you, Aleksei sent into Sheridan's thoughts.

He palmed her breast with one hand, while his other one reached between her legs to find her damp with desire. The musky smell of her passion drove him crazy. He licked her essence off his fingers before going back for more.

As he teased her clitoris, she began to pant. He pushed a finger into her wet heat. She gasped and then moaned as his fingers pressed deeper into her tight flesh. Her hand on his shaft, she pumped lightly, eroding his control. His wolf lifted its head, demanding a claiming. She squeezed him tighter. He couldn't last much longer.

Moving over her, he took her lips even as he lined himself up to fill her.

Say you want me...

Yes, more than anything, Sheridan sent telepathically.

"You are mine!" Aleksei declared.

He filled her completely, pushing deep. She pulsed around him, squeezing him tightly. He groaned.

Are you okay?

More than okay. Don't stop now...

Never.

Aleksei pulled back and then filled her again. Over and over, the pressure built. Desire unlike any he had felt before filled them. It flowed back and forth through the heartmate bond. Sheridan pushed up and wrapped her legs around his waist, trying to take him deeper.

Aleksei could no longer distinguish what pleasure was his or hers. The heartmate bond grew wider and glowed between them.

Come with me, baby.

As if his voice was the spark, they both detonated, merging and flying into the ether. Sheridan cried out. Aleksei buried his face in her neck and nipped her. Then he licked over the sting. She was his. His mate, forever.

§

The Christmas party was tonight. There were ten Shadow Walker guards on the property and some of Joe and Penny's family members would be present. However, Aleksei's parents and sisters were on a cruise in Alaska and his older brother, Tiernan was stationed with the Shadow Walkers in Washington D.C. He couldn't wait to tell them about his new mate.

Both, Aleksei and Daven would be circulating tonight, as well as Joe. Ben worked upstairs in the control room and just for tonight they had added some audio recorders. There was nowhere in the house that wasn't covered by some kind of electronic device, all of them feeding into the control room. Sheridan had delivered most of the food the day before and Penny's new cook worked at putting things out on trays.

Aleksei knew Sheridan would be showing up any time now and looked forward to seeing her. He took extra care with his outfit tonight. Of course, both he and Daven were dressed the same in tuxedos. They couldn't keep up the ruse without looking identical. He hoped to keep the confusion going as to whom was who to help ferret out the person behind the attacks. Luckily, the bruising was mostly gone from Daven's nose and Penny concealed the rest with a little makeup.

Everyone had kept the plan for this evening a secret. Aleksei hadn't even told Sheridan they hoped to flush out Daven's assailant tonight. He wasn't sure she would want her party to be used in such a way and he didn't want to worry her. Besides, Sheridan was so open that anyone looking at her could see what she was thinking. If she looked worried and concerned all night the party would be a failure.

Aleksei made sure there were pockets of shadow in each room. He wanted to make sure a Shadow Walker could walk in or out of each room without concern. The effect was very romantic with each light on a dimmer they had lowered to half way. Then Penny set out candles. Daven had teased both Penny and Sheridan about the kissing light so Sheridan went out and bought mistletoe for several of the corners and alcoves. Aleksei looked forward to catching Sheridan under the mistletoe.

Someone on the audio system crooned about a white Christmas when Sheridan walked through the front door. Aleksei stopped breathing. She wore a burgundy velvet dress that was off the shoulder and showed way too much skin for Aleksei's peace of mind. Her russet hair was up with a decorative comb and one loose curl lay on her neck. Aleksei's fingers itched to play with the curl and pull out the comb to let her hair cover those lovely shoulders. As if she could read his thoughts she walked into his waiting arms.

"Mess with that comb and no doggy treats for you, mister."

"You look good enough to eat. Who needs doggie treats?" Aleksei teased her. He had shared over the phone one night how his mother used to let him eat dog biscuits. Peanut butter was his childhood favorite but only in wolf form.

"I've got to get the food out. Jeffrey and Sara will be here as well as Jeffrey's little sister, Joanna."

"I've already informed the gate guard to let them in," Aleksei said, as he followed her into the kitchen. She put her purse and keys in the cupboard and Aleksei couldn't help but swoop in for a kiss. She kissed him back but then pushed at his chest. He reluctantly released her.

"Aleksei, I've got to get to work. If I get behind now, I'll be behind all night," she reprimanded him. "Go do some security something or other. Don't give me those puppy dog eyes—this is my job."

Aleksei turned to go but couldn't resist holding her hand until the last possible minute. He heard Sheridan laugh softly and felt a glow in his heart.

He went out the front door to find Joe standing at the bottom of the steps in a tuxedo. Joe looked sharp but clothes could never cover Joe's strict military bearing. Anyone looking at him would know he worked security.

"Our parents are coming along with our aunt Katherine," Joe grumbled. "I can't be worrying about them, I'll be out here unless you need me."

"Don't you like your Aunt Katherine?" Aleksei asked

"She's my favorite Aunt. But when she sees me, she calls me Joey and I feel like I'm six years old," Joe explained.

"Family can do that," Aleksei said, trying not to laugh at Joe's obvious distress.

They had become more than just employer/employee, they had become friends. Aleksei left Joe to check the people arriving against the guest list.

§

Sheridan bought a new dress for this party. She and Alek talked every night but she missed him. They had only been together twice in the last twelve days and both times Penny and Daven had been there. Sheridan liked Penny but she still didn't understand what she saw in Daven except his good looks.

She drove her little sedan up to the house. Joe stood outside. He walked over and opened her door for her. When she stepped out he smiled.

"You look gorgeous, Sheridan. Aleksei won't be able to keep his hands off you," he said, with a wink.

A uniformed valet came to take her car around the side to park.

"He better keep his hands to himself. I'm working tonight just like you," she answered with a smile.

"I'm sure the party will be a huge success," Joe said, as she walked up to the door. "It's open, go ahead on in."

"Thanks, Joe."

She stepped into the house and saw Aleksei coming down the stairs. He dressed in a tuxedo and looked like he walked out of a man's fashion magazine. Sheridan felt her breath catch when she looked into his eyes. He definitely liked what he saw when he looked at her. Sheridan was glad she bought the dress. He kept looking at her shoulders. She smiled.

He held his arms open and Sheridan willingly walked into them. It felt so good to be held in his arms, like coming home after a long day. She leaned in to catch a whiff of his scent. She couldn't get enough of his smell and moved closer.

"Keep that up and we'll be late to the party," he growled.

Sheridan laughed and turned toward the kitchen. He followed her but after a few minutes, he left so she could get to work.

The cook pulled out a tray of the bacon wrapped water chestnuts. Sheridan started making up platters. There was to be a large buffet in the dining room. Sheridan wanted to have some smaller trays for the coffee table in the living room.

The bar would be set up in the corner of the dining room. Sheridan had already prepared the site but she didn't know who Penny had hired to tend it. Daven had splurged on enough champagne for everyone to have a glass for a champagne toast when he announced his marriage and when the board announced his appointment as CEO. Sheridan thought it was a nice touch, but a bit extravagant. She moved from room to room, checking to make sure all was ready when a young man walked into the dining room wearing a festive red jacket.

"Hi, I'm Sheridan Harbrook the event planner," she said, arranging food on the platters next to the bar.

"Hi, I'm the bartender. Call me, Jack."

"Okay Jack, the wine and mixed drinks are for anyone who wants it. The champagne is for a special champagne toast, when Mr. McCloud is officially appointed CEO. I'll let you know when to start preparing it. If you need help, someone on my staff will be available to help you out."

"Sounds good, Miss Harbrook," Jack answered, cheerfully.

Sheridan watched for a few moments but it seemed like Jack knew what he was doing. She got back to preparing the food, the puff pastry with spinach still needed to be pulled out of the oven.

Sheridan was in the kitchen when the doorbell rang. She peered around the corner and saw Penny opening the door. Sheridan thought she looked lovely in her emerald green taffeta gown. With Penny willing to play hostess, it would give her more freedom to see to the smooth running of the party.

Just then Jeffrey, Sara, and Joanna walked into the kitchen. Sheridan started giving instructions and platters to Sara and Joanna to carry from room to room.

§

Aleksei hated parties. He tried to circulate and check for possible threats but every room he went into someone tried to waylay him. He had been propositioned twice already and the night was still young.

Daven seemed to be enjoying himself talking to the board members and flirting with their wives. Aleksei didn't think any of them were younger than sixty. Aleksei had stopped to chat with Penny's parents, Joe and Jessica. Now that there were three generations of Shadow Walkers, marriage between families became complicated. Aleksei wondered if anyone at Isanti kept track of tribal marriages and blood lines. He'd ask about it once this job was finished.

Aleksei had only seen Sheridan for a few minutes here and there. Last time he saw her, she looked a little hot and rumpled. Some of her curls had escaped the comb and were lying gently against her nape. Aleksei wanted to follow those curls with his lips but couldn't reach her before she was off again. The only thing that helped was she always looked for him when she entered the room. Their eyes would meet and she would give him a little smile, before attending to whatever needed to be done next.

Aleksei checked in with Joe and Ben every fifteen minutes. So far everything seemed quiet. Aleksei wondered if Daven's plan would work after all. He glanced at his watch and realized it had been almost two hours. If the intruder would strike, he must be here already.

"Joe, has everyone on the guest list arrived?"

"Yes, the last person arrived twenty minutes ago."

"Who was it? And I think you better close the gate," Aleksei said, with a feeling of foreboding.

"Charles Adams, he is the son of Sylvester Adams. He was on the guest list and his identification matched."

"Have Ben see if he can find him on the cameras and keep an eye on him. The champagne toast is going to be in a few minutes," Aleksei said, seeing the bartender Penny hired and Jeffrey pouring champagne into glasses and sending trays around the room.

Daven tried to get people's attention to say a few words and introduce Sylvester Adams. Aleksei saw Sheridan enter the room and begin to help pass out more glasses of champagne.

Aleksei could feel tension in the room, his wolf screaming of danger but he couldn't figure out why. *What was setting his wolf off?*

Aleksei turned to look around again. Sheridan walked toward him with two glasses of champagne. Daven went on and on about Mr. Adams the former president of the board.

Sheridan smiled and took a drink of the champagne. Her face changed from pleasure to horror. She dropped the glasses and grabbed her throat. Aleksei ran toward her but it seemed like everything moved in slow motion. Aleksei started telepathing mental instructions.

Joe, there's poison in the champagne. I'm not sure if it's in all of it or just mine.

Penny don't let anyone drink the champagne.

Ben did anyone tamper with the champagne?

Joe secure the exits, I want this guy caught.

Dr. Rick, I have an emergency. Poisoning. Coming in, now.

Aleksei finally reached Sheridan. She gasped for breath and then fainted into his arms. Aleksei smelled burnt almonds.

Cyanide, he sent.

Moving toward a dark corner in the room, he Shadow Walked to New Mexico and the infirmary with Sheridan in his arms. He walked out of Shadow and almost stumbled.

Dr. Rick and the nurses were waiting and pulled Sheridan out of his arms and rushed off with her. Aleksei couldn't breathe. He started to black out and sank down on a chair. Raven, was suddenly in his face, shaking him.

"Aleksei you need to fight the feelings of the drug. You're getting it from your mate. She's the one having a hard time breathing. Stay with me. Aleksei! You need to give Sheridan your strength. They're pumping her stomach and hopefully they'll get it all. You need to hold her here, Aleksei. If you don't we could lose both of you."

Aleksei tried to focus but he felt a wave of terror rising. Raven talked about losing Sheridan.

No! He couldn't lose her.

Then Sheridan felt his fear through the mating bond. She actually tried to calm him. He grabbed on to her essence and poured his love into the link.

Sending her strength through the heartmate bond, he sheltered her from the pain and violation of pumping her stomach. Aleksei felt the IV as it was placed in her arm as well as the tube down her throat.

He wrapped his mind around hers and held on tight. She was weak but she fought against it. Aleksei sent her more of his strength. He looked up at Raven with so many questions but he didn't dare speak or move. It took all of his concentration to protect Sheridan from the experiences her body went through.

"Don't worry, everyone else is okay," Raven assured him. "Joe has everything under control. You need to have all your concentration on your mate. We'll take care of the rest."

Aleksei closed his eyes and concentrated on Sheridan. He held her gently in his mind. He wasn't sure how to help but wanted her to feel safe. So, he sent her his memories of the day they had played in the yard. He shared the joy of running and the fun of playing. The triumph of winning, and the love behind all his wolf kisses. He could feel her awareness of the memories and of Aleksei holding her in his mind.

Aleksei?

I have you, Sherry. Hang onto me, my love.

I feel so strange. What is happening?

Trust me, love. Just rest here and remember all the good times we've had. Did you have fun running in the yard?

Being with you always makes me happy.

Aleksei could feel Sheridan growing weaker. He held her harder now, afraid of losing her. His wolf howled in agony and the whole tribe heard the echo through the tribal link.

Then Aleksei felt his mother and father link with him and send him their strength and love. He felt Raven place a hand on his shoulder and add to the link. Then others joined. His grandfather, Isanti, linked with the others. They fed all the strength and love of the tribe into Aleksei, who in turn fed it to Sheridan. Then Aleksei felt Joe and Penny join the link, and then Penny's parents, Ben and Brad, and countless others.

Sheridan sighed in his mind. Her strength slowly returning, she lay quietly, soaking up the tremendous love and strength of the tribe. Aleksei was pretty sure the danger had passed but held onto the link.

Then something strange and wonderful happened. The love grew, it doubled, and tripled. It spread out to each member of the tribe, expanding, and renewing. It continued to grow, and more, and more people joined the link. Mothers linked with their children, husbands with their wives. It grew larger and stronger.

Aleksei felt Daven join the link and then he felt Sheridan pull her mother into the link. The love continued to grow until all of the souls became one with all. The entire tribe basked in unconditional love. Sheridan glowed so brightly, the nurses had to avert their eyes.

Dr. Frederick "Rick" White Fox ran out to see Aleksei glowing just like his mate.

"What is going on here?" He questioned, and the question flowed through the link, breaking the spell.

People started to blink and fall out of the link. Others lingered not wanting the feeling to go away. But they were aware of their separation again and soon drifted away. Finally, it came down to Aleksei's family. They sent mental caresses and broke the link as well.

Aleksei opened his eyes as Dr. Rick walked up.

"I think you should come back and see your mate now. She's resting comfortably."

Aleksei and Raven followed Dr. Rick into the examination room. Sheridan sat up in bed, looking radiant and relaxed. Aleksei rushed to her and crushed her to his chest. Then he kissed her, first her mouth, and then her face. Finally, he leaned his forehead on hers and shuddered.

§

Raven reached telepathically for his wife, Cara. He could feel that she had been crying recently.

It was so beautiful, she sent sensing her husband's concern.

What just happened? Raven sent.

It was Sheridan, she is a healer, an emotional healer. She has some kind of empathic gift and can use emotions to heal with. She and Aleksei are a potent combination. He is like you and Isanti, a kind of hub. He can link with everyone in the tribe down to the youngest child. They are both more powerful than anyone and together more powerful than all of us.

Raven looked over to see Aleksei and Sheridan wrapped in each other's arms. Shudders racked Aleksei's frame.

"I almost lost you," Aleksei said.

"I'm here," Sheridan answered.

Raven stepped from the room giving the couple some privacy. He knew the shock of the evening hit hard. Aleksei and the members of the tribe that had wolf spirits were small in number but great in spirit. At one time they would have been seen as something sacred. Now they were family you made allowances for.

Isanti appeared from the shadows. He seemed to be getting thinner, his face lined with age and his silver braids shinning in the light. He stood next to his foster son and peered into the room.

"I came to check on my grandson," Isanti explained, looking through the doorway to where Aleksei and Sheridan lay on the bed in each other's arms. "I see right now he is all consumed with his mate," he said, with a chuckle "I will approach him later, goodnight children." And then he smiled at Raven and disappeared into Shadow.

Raven laughed. Isanti always made a big entrance, and big exit, wherever he went.

§

Sheridan leaned into Aleksei's chest. It always felt so good to be held in his arms. She still felt a little disoriented with everything that had happened tonight. But could still feel the unconditional love at the core of her being. If she tried, Sheridan could find others who had been in the telepathic link. It was as if a pathway had been created that led to everyone in the tribe. But all the paths started with Aleksei and that was fine with her. Aleksei was her everything. Sheridan wasn't sure how they would manage it but Aleksei was her life, as she was his.

She looked up as the doctor came over.

"Can Alek stay here?" Sheridan asked.

"I'm sure he wouldn't have it any other way," Dr. Rick said, chuckling. "You know he bit me once when he was a pup. I tried to pull porcupine quills out of his leg and paw. He didn't take it well. All I need is your arm, Sheridan, for a blood sample. I think you should stay on the premises tonight."

"I'll need to call my mother and let her know."

"I'll send someone with a phone."

"Thank you, doctor," Sheridan said but he was already hurrying out the door.

Sheridan snuggled back into Aleksei's arms. He lay completely on the bed, stretched out beside her. He watched her with so much love in his eyes that she felt an answering glow in her heart.

"Will you marry me, Sherry? I love you more than life itself."

Tears of joy came to her eyes. "Yes. I love you with all my heart."

"I'm sorry I don't have a ring to give you, and this isn't the most romantic setting..." Sheridan placed her fingers on his lips.

"This is perfect. You saved my life, tonight. Then we shared our minds and souls with the whole tribe. It was a miracle. The rest will fall into place."

Aleksei leaned down and kissed her with gentleness and love. Sheridan kissed him back.

Someone cleared their throat at the door. They both looked up to see Joe. He had a black eye.

"Sorry to interrupt," he said, "but I thought you would want a report before the night was out. Charles Adams, and the bartender, Jack Simpson, are now in custody and charged with multiple counts of attempted murder. The hidden camera in the dining room caught them exchanging a small bottle that we later found stashed under the bar. It was cyanide like you thought. The police want your statements, once Sheridan is well enough, of course. We had to explain that you were in a private, secure care facility, and would be available tomorrow. Of course, we didn't mention you were in New Mexico. Everyone else is fine. The champagne was taken into evidence and the party dispersed with the arrival of the police. Before that, the guests were unsure of a problem. I hope this doesn't hurt your business, Sheridan."

"I'm sure it will be fine, Joe," Sheridan said. "It might even bring in business. Are you okay? Your eye...."

"The bartender got in a lucky shot. I'm fine."

"Thanks, Joe," Aleksei said. "Please tell the team I said, 'great work' and put some ice on that eye."

"Sure thing, Boss," Joe said.

§

Christmas morning dawned cool and bright in California. A hush seemed to lay over the neighborhood. Sheridan grabbed her robe and then peeked in on her mother before making her way to the kitchen. She frowned at the lack of Christmas decorations. With all the decorating and party planning she'd done for Enchanted Evenings, she hadn't had time to put anything up here in her own home. Thank goodness she didn't have a party planned for tonight. She started some water to boil and reached for a cup when she heard knocking on the front door.

Frowning, Sheridan went to see who it was. She opened the door to see Aleksei. He looked festive wearing a red sweater and Santa hat perched on his head.

"Good morning, *milaya*. Merry Christmas."

"Alek, do you know what time it is?" Sheridan asked, stepping back and motioning him inside. She turned toward the kitchen assuming Aleksei would follow.

"Not awake yet? I brought you breakfast, fresh cinnamon scones. Your favorite."

The smell of cinnamon wafted from the box Aleksei held out to her.

"Thank you. I'm sorry I'm not all here yet. I just got up."

"No worries. You sit down and let me get your tea." Aleksei pushed her into one of the kitchen chairs. "Today, I'm taking care of you."

He stood behind her for a moment massaging her shoulders. Sheridan sighed in contentment. Suddenly, she heard the front door open and voices in the front room.

"Who can that be?" Sheridan asked.

"Uh, uhh. Stay here, I'll take care of it." Aleksei placed a mug of hot tea in front of her and went into the front room.

120

Sheridan listened to the voices and thought she heard Joe. *What are they up to now?* She sighed. Deciding to take Aleksei's advice, she reached for one of the scones. She took a big bite and moaned as the flavor hit her tongue.

"I love it when you make that sound," Aleksei said, from the doorway. "You make it hard for me to stick to my plan. Now all I want to do is take you to bed."

"What plan is that?" Sheridan asked, licking cinnamon off her fingers.

"For starters, your house needs a little Christmas cheer. I've already got that under control. Then after presents, I thought we could visit with my family for a little while. They'll want to feed us, so you don't have to worry about fixing Christmas dinner. Now, after you finish devouring that scone, you might want to get dressed."

"Alek, my mother..."

"We're taking her with us. Don't worry about a thing. I've hired a nurse to prepare your mother for our outing."

"I don't know what to say..."

"Go get dressed, Sherry, wear all-natural fibers."

Sheridan finished her tea and then went down the hall to her room. She tried not to peek at what was happening in the living room. She didn't want to ruin Aleksei's surprise.

After donning a pair of jeans and a sweater, she stood in front of the mirror in the bathroom. She fussed with her hair for a while but the extra time was more about walking back into the living room then how she looked.

Aleksei surprised her. He said he'd be coming over but they hadn't set a time. She smiled. Letting someone else plan the day might be a good idea. Didn't she want a man who would take care of her? A soft knock on the door made her jump.

"Stop hiding in the bathroom and come see what Santa brought you," Aleksei said.

Chapter Ten

Aleksei waited for Sheridan to open the bathroom door. The nurse had already helped her mother into the front room. He couldn't wait to see Sherry's reaction to the tree and pile of presents he'd arranged to be delivered.

She opened the door and gazed at him.

"You're having fun, aren't you?"

"You bet. Christmas is about giving and you are the one I want to see happy."

"Come here and kiss me," Sheridan said, grabbing him. He obliged her request with a smile and a kiss to knock her socks off.

"Better?" he asked, when he pulled back.

"Merry Christmas, Aleksei," Sheridan said, brushing her fingers over his jaw.

"Merry Christmas, *lyubov moya*." Aleksei led Sheridan down the hall and into the front room.

She gasped. "It's beautiful. I can't believe you bought such a large tree and managed to decorate it so quickly."

"Well, he did have some help," Joe said, walking in from the kitchen. He held a mug of steaming liquid in his hand. "Ben and Brad send their Christmas greetings. They returned home to help their parents."

"I'll have to send them a thank you card," Sheridan said.

"Later," Aleksei said, pulling her over to the couch. Sit, so I can play Santa." Aleksei started pulling packages from beneath the tree and placing them in front of Sheridan and her mother. He even had one for Joe, who raised an eyebrow at the offering.

"Alek, can you look in the bag by the front door. There's more presents in there," Sheridan said, her hands in her lap.

Aleksei grabbed the shopping bags in question and pulled out a present for Sheridan's mother and then...one for him. He smiled and rattled the box, listening for a clue of what might be inside.

"Hey, stop that," Sheridan scolded. "Go ahead and open it."

Aleksei ripped off the wrapping paper and then opened the box to find a blue silk tie with the picture of a black wolf on it.

"Wow. I love it." He looked at Sheridan. His chest warmed by the tenderness in her gaze. He rolled the tie and put it on the end table.

"Your turn, Joe," Sheridan said.

They all turned to watch as Joe carefully removed the bow, unwrapped the paper on the box without a single tear, folded it, and then opened the lid. He pulled out an Isanti polo shirt with "Joe Running Bear" and "Head of Security" embroidered on the front.

"Thanks, Boss," he said quietly, folding the shirt and returning it to the box.

"You deserve it, my friend," Aleksei said, smiling.

They all turned to watch as Sheridan helped her mother open her presents and then it was Sheridan's turn. Aleksei was so excited it was hard to sit still.

Sheridan opened the snow boots first, then the down jacket, and finally the knitted wool hat, scarf, and mittens.

"Everything is Shadow Walker safe," he explained, handing her the snow boots.

"We're still going to your parent's house?" she asked, pulling on the boots.

"Yes, we are, but I thought it might be fun to build a snowman outside when we get there. But before we go, I have one last present..." Aleksei pulled a ring box out of his pocket and got down on one knee. "I know I asked before but I wanted to do it properly with this." He held the box out to her. "Will you marry me?"

"You know I will," Sheridan said, opening the box. She gasped and her hand shook. "It's beautiful..." She blinked back tears.

Aleksei rose and pulled the four-carat solitaire diamond ring from the box and placed it on her ring finger, sealing it with a kiss.

"I just want you to know, I have witnesses that you said 'yes.' You're mine!"

"You are such a wolf," Sheridan whispered.

"You better believe it, baby," Aleksei said, holding Sheridan in his arms.

"Joe, if you will escort Sheridan's mother to the party?"

"On it," Joe said. He leaned down to speak to the older woman. It wasn't long until they disappeared into a shadow.

"I hope you don't mind," Aleksei said, "I wanted a moment alone with you. I have a huge family and an even bigger extended family. Once we Shadow Walk to Montana, we'll be lucky to stay in the same room, let alone have time together."

"That sounds intriguing. Will they tell me all your secrets?" Sheridan asked. Aleksei handed her the jacket and hat.

"I'm sure every embarrassing moment of my life will be shared with glee." Aleksei shook his head. "Just remember I love you, and you said you'd marry me." He handed her the mittens and then put the scarf around her neck, using it to pull her in for a kiss.

"I won't forget," Sheridan whispered.

§

That evening, after Shadow Walking back to California, and putting her mother to bed, Sheridan stared at the lights on the Christmas tree and sighed. *What a wonderful day.* Someone sang about being warmer in the winter on the stereo. Sheridan smiled.

It was like someone had a list of the best Christmas activities and they had marked all the entries off, snow, caroling, cookies, snowball fight, a roaring fire, kissing under the mistletoe, family, good food, and fun.

"Here," Aleksei said, walking into the room holding two mugs. "Hot chocolate."

Sheridan giggled.

"What's so funny?" Aleksei asked.

"I was just going over our day. Hot chocolate was the only thing missing from my list." She took the mug and sipped the chocolaty goodness.

"What list?"

"The Best Activities for a Perfect Christmas list. Thank you for today."

"Today was just the beginning, Sherry. Every day is perfect when you're with me."

New Year's Eve

Aleksei walked into the party and quickly scanned the crowd looking for Sheridan. He finally found her standing near the buffet table talking to Jeffrey. She glanced up at that moment and saw him. It was like the whole world ceased to exist in that instant. They were the only two people in the whole world.

"You're late," she mouthed even as she smiled at him.

Now, if he could just get through the throng of people. As he walked, he admired the purple, silver, and black embellishments Sheridan used to decorate. This party would be another success Sherry could add to her portfolio.

Trays of champagne began to circulate around the room as everyone prepared for the clock to strike twelve. Sheridan patted Jeffrey's arm and walked around the buffet table on her way to intercepting him.

They met near the middle of the dance floor. Aleksei gladly pulled her into his arms.

126

"I'm sorry, I'm late. I had to stop by your house and see your mother."

"Is everything all right?"

"I brought her flowers and visited with her and her nurses."

"You're so sweet, nobody would believe you're a wolf."

"Why not? Wolves are loyal, trustworthy, and protective of their own," Aleksei said, dipping her to the crowds delight. "I love you, Sheridan and I always will."

"I love you too, Aleksei."

"Good, then I have a surprise for you. Your mother and I decided a Valentine's Day wedding would be very romantic."

"You think so?"

"I do, and to save you the trouble, I've already got people working on it. Unless you want to elope then we could run up to Vegas."

"Aleksei..." Sheridan laughed. "What am I going to do with you."

"I know I'm taking over but you do enough event planning for work. I wanted to give you something special.

"You are giving me something special," Sheridan said, throwing her arms around his neck. "You're giving me yourself. I love you."

The Master of Ceremonies began to count down to midnight and the crowd joined in... "Five, Four, Three, Two, One...Happy New Year!"

"Happy New Year, darling," Sheridan whispered.

Aleksei pulled her close and kissed her. *Happy New Year, lyubov moya.*

Sheridan let Aleksei sweep her around the dance floor. Joy filled her. The man of her dreams held her in his arms. The party progressed and the evening was wonderful.

"I'd like to steal you away, I hope you don't mind."

"Aleksei, I have to help clean up," Sheridan said, her joy dimming.

"I already talked to Jeffrey and Joanna. They said they would handle things."

"Ah, a conspiracy..." Sheridan smiled, intrigued.

"No, just people who love you. Come on, I see a shadow over in that corner."

Sheridan shivered as the cold and dark of the Shadow Dimension enveloped her. She might have panicked but Aleksei held her close in his arms. She stumbled as they walked back into the light.

"My shoes?"

Sheridan looked down at her stockinged feet on the luxurious carpet of the hotel suite they now occupied.

"Sorry about that. They weren't made of all-natural materials."

"Is that why you sent the sexy lingerie? I didn't realize it was more than a ploy to get me into bed."

Sheridan walked over to the large king-sized bed in the room. Rose petals lined the sheets and candles glowed from the night stands.

"Did it work, because getting you into bed is exactly what I had planned."

"I can see that," Sheridan said, running her finger lightly over a petal.

She looked over to see Aleksei already had his coat off and his shirt unbuttoned. Her fingers began to itch to touch his chest and rub her fingers down the grooves in his abs. *He is so beautiful.*

He kicked off his shoes and removed his belt. Her nipples began to harden and a flush of warmth settled in her core.

"You'll have to help me with this zipper," she said, her voice coming out breathy.

"It will be a pleasure," Aleksei said, his eyes flashing golden showing his wolf was close to the surface.

A wave of desire made her knees weak. Sheridan reached for one of the posts of the bed as she turned her back to him. He slowly pulled the zipper of her purple velvet dress down, kissing her shoulders and neck. Then he reached up and removed the silver comb from her hair.

Sheridan sighed and leaned back against him as he pushed the dress off her shoulders and it fell to the floor.

She stepped out of the garment and stood before him in the white lace ensemble he'd sent. She especially liked the silk stockings and garter belt, though the corset was a little uncomfortable, it did nice things for her figure.

Aleksei stared, his gaze drinking her in.

"You're the most beautiful woman I've ever seen."

"You don't go to the movies much do you?"

"Even if I did, it wouldn't change my mind."

"Why don't you take off the rest of your clothes and then you can come help me." Sheridan sat on the bed and crossed one knee over the other, striking a pose. "I had to ask Penny to help me get into this contraption."

"Remind me to thank her later," Aleksei said, reaching for the zipper of his pants.

It was now Sheridan's turn to stare. *I am so lucky.*

"Like what you see?" Aleksei asked.

"Absolutely."

He chuckled. "Let's see if I can get you untied."

Aleksei worked at loosening the laces of the corset so Sheridan could take it off.

"If I knew this would be so difficult, I wouldn't have bought it."

"Don't be that way. Sometimes, unwrapping a gift is the best part."

Aleksei kissed her shoulder. "All finished, *lyubov moya.*"

Sheridan removed the corset and reached for the silk stockings.

"Let me," Aleksei said, kneeling before her.

He unbuckled the stocking from the garter belt and began to roll it down her leg, his lips following in its wake. By the time his lips kissed her ankle, she trembled.

He smiled and reached for the second stocking, his knuckles brushing against her panties. Sheridan gasped.

Aleksei watched her face as he gave her second thigh, leg, and ankle the same kisses as the first. Sheridan sank to the edge of the bed, her legs too weak to hold her. Aleksei shifted forward and grabbed the edge of the lace thong. With a twist of his wrist it broke and he pulled it off.

"You ruined the set," she said, her voice hoarse with desire.

"I bought an extra thong so I could do just that."

He lifted her leg and put it over his shoulder before lowering his head to lick up her slit.

Sheridan groaned and fell back on the bed. Aleksei pulled her closer to the edge and began to lick her in earnest. He growled as he did, the vibration making her tremble harder.

He speared his tongue into her core and Sheridan almost leapt from the bed.

"Aleksei, you're killing me..."

You like it, whispered into her mind.

Yes, yes, she did. Desire flowed through the mating bond as her pleasure increased. Her fingers tangled in the bedcovers. She needed to hold on to something. Her head thrashed to and fro.

Let go, sweetheart. I've got you.

Aleksei moved his mouth to her clit and slipped a finger inside her. He bent the digit so it scraped against her flesh. Sheridan exploded. Pleasure, love, ecstasy swept her away.

"Alek!" she screamed. Her vision dimmed.

Epilogue: Christmas one year later

Sheridan closed the door to her mother's room. With tears in her eyes, she turned to leave the house for the last time. She had hoped to have her mother with her a little longer but it wasn't meant to be. At least her mother had lived long enough to see Sheridan get married. The last year had been the happiest her mother had experienced in her final four. Sheridan walked down the stone path and into Aleksei's arms.

Are you all right, Sherry?

This is so hard, Aleksei. I feel a little lost.

I have you, love. Your mother is still with us in spirit. She will work with the Great Spirit to see that our child has a good life. Reach for her through your link. Can you not still feel her love for you.

How is that possible? I do still feel her love.

We are not truly alone but one with all things. The energy that is your mother's spirit is still alive and connected to us. Come, love, we need to go.

Sheridan let Aleksei lead her to the car and help her in. She took one last look at the little ranch house she had shared with her mother and the "For Sale" and "Under Contract" signs in the front yard. Aleksei pulled out of the driveway and drove toward Daven and Penny's estate.

Daven and Penny worked hard to turn McCloud Industries around and it now was turning a sizable profit. Sylvester Adams had sold his company shares to Daven and fled to Florida and retirement after the embarrassment of his son's crimes. Sheridan still could not believe the hatred Charles felt toward Daven for replacing his father as CEO.

131

Sheridan sold her business to Joseph and his sister, Joanna. She was sure they would make a success of it. She looked forward to having her evenings free to spend with Aleksei. She really wasn't a party girl at heart.

When her mother had passed away quietly in her sleep, Sheridan didn't know how to feel. She was relieved her mother would no longer suffer but angry that *now* that she didn't have to worry about money and her mother's care, her mother had left her. Grief hit people in strange ways.

Finding Aleksei turned her world upside down but she had never been happier, even with her mother's passing. She wasn't alone anymore and knew she was truly loved and cherished by Aleksei and the wolf that shared his spirit. He reached over and squeezed her hand.

They had already had two surprises this week. First, her mother's house had sold, and secondly, she carried their first child. Sheridan wondered what other surprises were in store as they pulled into Daven's drive and waited for the gate to open.

As they drove up to the house, Sheridan saw the topiaries were lined up and the wreaths were on the door and windows. She smiled at the festive display.

Penny and Daven stood on the front porch in each other's arms. Aleksei pulled the car up and parked, then rushed around to help Sheridan out of the vehicle. He was very protective of his pregnant wife.

"I am not going to break, Aleksei," Sheridan said, rolling her eyes.

"Let me care for you, mate," Aleksei grumbled.

Sheridan laughed and let Aleksei tuck her into his side, something he did frequently. He seemed to need the physical contact and Sheridan felt treasured by his actions. He sniffed the air and looked around, always on alert.

"Sheridan, Aleksei, we have news," Penny said, as they walked up the front steps.

Everyone exchanged a hug and then Penny ushered them inside the foyer.

"I'm so excited, I can't wait to tell you. We're pregnant, too. Our children will be able to grow up best friends," Penny said, almost bouncing with her enthusiasm.

More hugs and handshakes were exchanged as everyone walked into the front room.

"Penny decorated the house with the decorations from the party last year, except this year we have fake garlands," Daven said, proudly.

"What do you think of Winnie the Pooh for the nursery?" Penny asked.

She and Sheridan were soon off on a tangent about colors and themes for the children's rooms.

Aleksei looked at Daven and they both got up to go into the library. A little tree sat in the corner decorated with the items Sheridan had used last year. Aleksei fingered one of the burgundy balls while flashes of Sheridan and the last year went through his mind. Daven poured himself a scotch and they both took a chair in front of the fire.

"I never would have believed you if, last year after I called, you said that we would be married and having children," Daven admitted.

"It was a surprise for me as well," Aleksei said. "Now that I have Sheridan in my life, I cannot be happy without her."

"I feel the same way about Penny. She brings me such joy. Are you going to take over as CEO of Isanti, Inc?"

"I'm not sure, yet. Sheridan is still dealing with the death of her mother and we now have the excitement of the baby coming. I may wait another year. Uncle Raven isn't going anywhere."

"No, I suppose he isn't." Daven chuckled.

Aleksei raised his scotch. "Here's to our Christmas miracles, our wives, and our unborn children," Aleksei said, with a smile and feeling of joy in his heart. He caught an echo as Sheridan felt his joy and added her love into the mating bond.

He smiled. *Ah, life is good.*

§§§

Coming Soon

Terrene Magic
Book Five of the Witch Guardian Romance Series

Tricked into falling through a dimensional portal, Chelsea Amhurst soon discovers that life is more than being the daughter of the Speaker of the Witch's Council and flirting with the good-looking Guardians that work for her father. She will need to pull on all of her magical reserves in order to find her way home.

Seth MacDonald may be the youngest member of the Witch Guardian Police Force, but being a Lycan gives him benefits that his fellow witch members don't have. For one, most magic doesn't affect him when in his Lycan form. When he finds himself and his future mate, Chelsea, in another dimension, he will need every one of his Lycan gifts to keep them alive.

Rurik
Book Two of The Volkov Family Chronicles

Starr Conrad is a Supernatural hiding in New York City. She is also a police officer using her gifts to give justice to the people. During a call, she is targeted by a sniper and saved by a Good Samaritan who is wounded. Something about the man calls to her. Her heart actually aches with the intensity of desire that hits her. She summons medical assistance for the civilian, but needs to report to her commanding officer. When she comes back to find her hero... He's gone and she's left with a grief so strong she's not sure she will survive its intensity.

Rurik Volkov is the heir to the Siberian Lycan Pack Alpha. But at the moment, he is helping his sister and new brother-in-law while they assume the duties of the New York City Alphas. Someone is manufacturing a neurotoxin that kills Shifters called Manna Dust and the Supernatural community must find out who. While helping, he is shot protecting a woman police officer. Imagine his surprise when the lycan mating bond snaps into place. Now he must find who is targeting Supernaturals before they are all killed, while somehow convincing Officer Conrad to be his mate, not to mention move to Siberia.

Also by Caryn Moya Block/Caryn Block

The Siberian Volkov Romance Series

Alpha's Mate

A Siberian Werewolf in London

My Mate's Embrace

My Magic Mate

A Siberian Werewolf in Paris

A Siberian Werewolf Christmas

Wolfe's Mate

Beta's Mate

The Gift of My Mate

My Perfect Mate

Shadow Mate

Lycan's Mate

The Witch Guardian Fantasy Romance Series

Destined Magic

Aerial Magic

Fiery Magic

Aqua Magic

Coming Soon

Terrene Magic

The Shadow Walker Tribe Romance Series

Shadow of My Heart

Love in the Shadows

Black and Shadow

Trapped in Shadow

Cross-Over Novels – Shadow Mate

Lycan's Mate

The Volkov Family Chronicles

Katya

Coming Soon

Rurik

<u>The Shadow Walker-Lycan Hybrid Second Generation Stories</u>

Christmas Shadow

Coming Soon

The Three Graces

<u>The Enlighten Up Series</u>

Joy, My Journey of Awakening

<u>The Psychic Kid's Series</u>

Feelings Not My Own

I See Spirits

My First Reiki Book

Rainbow Lights

About the Author

In January of 2012, Caryn Moya Block began her writing career with the debut of *Alpha's Mate* which won the "Global E-book Award for 2012" in contemporary romance. She was also named one of the "Top 50 Indie Authors for April 2012" from E-Reader Reviews. Her novel, *A Siberian Werewolf in Paris,* was chosen as a paranormal category finalist in the 2014 RomCon.com Readers' Choice Awards.

Caryn continues to write, giving her readers five different series to choose from: *The Shadow Walkers Romance Series, The Witch Guardian Romance Series*, and the very popular, *Siberian Volkov Pack Romance Series*. She has just begun the second-generation character books with *The Volkov Family Chronicles Series* and *The Shadow Walker- Lycan Hybrid Second Generation Series*.

She also has four children's books published under the name, Caryn Block, and has an adult non-fiction book, *Joy, My Journey of Awakening*.

Caryn loves romantic movies and stories that end "Happily Ever After." She lives in Virginia with her pack which consists of her husband of more than thirty years, two grown sons, two beautiful daughters-in-law, three granddaughters, and two Shetland sheepdogs. She suffers from "Multiple Sheltie Syndrome," because "one is never enough."

After seeing her first ghost when she was three years old, Caryn has continued to be intrigued with the paranormal.

She would love to hear from you at: CarynMoyaBlock@gmail.com

Sign up for her newsletter at: http://carynmoyablock.com

www.ingramcontent.com/pod-product-compliance
Lightning Source LLC
Chambersburg PA
CBHW050758250626
47155CB00005B/2125